ONE HOT DESERT NIGHT

—

KRISTI GOLD

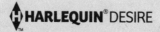

If you purchased this book without a cover you should be aware that this book is stolen property. It was reported as "unsold and destroyed" to the publisher, and neither the author nor the publisher has received any payment for this "stripped book."

Recycling programs
for this product may
not exist in your area.

ISBN-13: 978-0-373-73363-7

One Hot Desert Night

Copyright © 2015 by Kristi Goldberg

All rights reserved. Except for use in any review, the reproduction or utilization of this work in whole or in part in any form by any electronic, mechanical or other means, now known or hereinafter invented, including xerography, photocopying and recording, or in any information storage or retrieval system, is forbidden without the written permission of the publisher, Harlequin Enterprises Limited, 225 Duncan Mill Road, Don Mills, Ontario M3B 3K9, Canada.

This is a work of fiction. Names, characters, places and incidents are either the product of the author's imagination or are used fictitiously, and any resemblance to actual persons, living or dead, business establishments, events or locales is entirely coincidental.

This edition published by arrangement with Harlequin Books S.A.

For questions and comments about the quality of this book, please contact us at CustomerService@Harlequin.com.

® and TM are trademarks of Harlequin Enterprises Limited or its corporate affiliates. Trademarks indicated with ® are registered in the United States Patent and Trademark Office, the Canadian Intellectual Property Office and in other countries.

Printed in U.S.A.

Kristi Gold has a fondness for beaches, baseball and bridal reality shows. She firmly believes that love has remarkable healing powers and feels very fortunate to be able to weave stories of love and commitment. As a bestselling author, a National Readers' Choice Award winner and a Romance Writers of America three-time RITA® Award finalist, Kristi has learned that although accolades are wonderful, the most cherished rewards come from networking with readers. She can be reached through her website at www.kristigold.com, or through Facebook.

Books by Kristi Gold

Harlequin Desire

The Return of the Sheikh
One Night with the Sheikh
From Single Mom to Secret Heiress
The Sheikh's Son
One Hot Desert Night

Visit Kristi Gold's profile at Harlequin.com for more titles.

To my future son-in-law, Christopher.
We are so blessed to have you in our family.

One

Sheikh Rayad Rostam had blood on his hands, a bounty on his head and a burden he had carried for years.

Though at times he longed for peace, he had lived on the edge for so long, he knew no other way. And today, as he stared out the palace window to the mountains towering over Bajul, the pain in his side reminding him of his recent face-off with possible death, his never-ending mission still urged him to continue.

"You cannot return to your duties until you are medically cleared, Rayad."

An order issued by the king, who happened to be his cousin. He despised any attempts to dictate his choices and a life where family loyalty and royal decrees prevailed. Battling anger, he chose to keep his attention focused on the familiar landscape to avoid Rafiq's scrutiny. "I do not see why I cannot return immediately. I have suffered much worse than broken ribs and will probably do so again."

"And the next time you could very well sustain wounds that will not heal, particularly if your cover was breached."

That sent him around to face Rafiq as he struggled to suppress his fury over the reminders of his downfall. A tragic event that had set his life-long course. "I learned from my mistake many years ago, and since that time no one has learned my identity. As far as my safety is concerned, that is a risk I take to fulfill my duty to this country."

Rafiq leaned back in the chair situated behind the massive desk and streaked a palm over his goatee, seemingly unaffected by the ire in Rayad's tone. "You go beyond the limits of risk-taking, cousin, as you continue your futile quest for elusive killers that you will most likely never find."

Bordered on losing control, he braced his palms on the edge of the desk and leaned forward. "I will never stop searching until I locate and punish those responsible."

Rafiq raised a brow. "And if you do not find them?"

He straightened, hands fisted at his sides. "I will die trying."

"And that, Rayad, is exactly what I fear will happen if you do not reassess your goals. I have accepted that I will never know the true circumstance behind my mother's death. I have also accepted Rima's death was no fault of my own."

"My situation is very different, Rafiq. You speak of a possible accident or suicide. I speak of murder."

"Some answers are not meant to be known, but life is meant to be lived. You should rebuild yours as I have. You should honor your royal heritage by continuing the legacy with an heir."

A concept that was not feasible in light of the tragedy that remained foremost on his mind. "Unlike you and your brothers, Rafiq, my duties prevent me from considering taking a wife and bearing children."

"I am ruler of our country," Rafiq said. "Zain has established a water-conservation system that will secure Bajul's future. Adan is the commander of our armed forces. We have all been successful in our endeavors to bear children and keep our wives satisfied."

Since Rayad's recent arrival at the royal palace, all signs pointed to that success every night during the evening meal when he had been subjected to several miniature Mehdis, and Maysa, the king's very pregnant wife. "I commend you on that achievement, Rafiq. However, I am personally not interested in attaining domestic tranquility."

Rafiq narrowed his eyes and studied him a lengthy moment. "Are you so lost in your thirst for revenge that you no longer crave the company of a woman?"

"I am not celibate, yet there are very few women I trust enough to bed."

"How long has it been since you have been with a woman, Rayad?"

Too long to admit to any other man. "I have been infiltrating several insurgent encampments for the past eight months, or do you not recall giving that directive?"

Rafiq released a rough sigh. "Perhaps you should take this opportunity and use it to locate a suitable mate."

He had heard the same suggestions from his parents, as if they expected him to discard the pain and remorse. Clearly, no one understood that he only wanted to sate his natural desire, not settle into an ordinary life. "Even if I consented to wed as you and my father suggest, suitable brides in Bajul are rare, Rafiq. Most are married or too young."

Rafiq scowled. "Must you make this so difficult? You are free to travel to another region if necessary. I am certain your father can locate prospects in Dubai."

In an effort to quell the subject, Rayad returned to the window where he glimpsed the official armored limousine arriving at the entrance. When the driver rounded the car and opened the door, a lithe woman exited the vehicle, the afternoon sun glinting off her long blond hair. Her clothing was somewhat conservative and nondescript, yet she moved with the grace of a gazelle. As she removed the sunshades covering her eyes and glanced up at the window where he now stood, Rayad was struck by her beauty, and immediately reminded of his unwelcome abstinence.

Forcing his gaze away, he regarded Rafiq over one shoulder. "Are you expecting a guest? Specifically a female guest?"

"That is accurate," Rafiq said. "She will be staying here for an indeterminate amount of time."

He thrust his hands in his pockets and slowly began to pace the area. "Is she wed?"

The king presented his best scowl. "No, she is not, but I caution you to stay away from her, Rayad."

He paused midstride and turned toward his suddenly irritable cousin. "Why? Are you interested in bedding her?"

"Of course not," Rafiq said. "If you recall, I have a bride."

He could not resist the urge to bait the king. "This is true, but perhaps you have decided to reinstate ancient customs and populate a harem."

Rafiq's venomous look revealed he did not appreciate the conjecture. "The woman is Adan's sister-in-law. Should you trifle with her, you will have to answer to him, your commander in chief, as well as Piper, his wife."

That did not deter Rayad from exploring all possibilities. "Does this woman have a name?"

"Sunny McAdams. She is an international correspondent, and I highly doubt she would be interested in engaging in a temporary affair with you, if that is what you are considering. It is my understanding she has recently dissolved a relationship with a colleague."

What better way to temporarily move past loss than with mutual passion? Of course, she would have to be willing. He had never taken from a woman what she refused to give. He never would. "I appreciate your counsel, cousin," he said as he backed toward the door.

"I assure you I will take your concerns into consideration." *And promptly ignore them.*

"That would be wise, Rayad, and I suggest…"

Rayad closed the door on the king before he had a chance to finish his lecture. At the moment, he intended to give the palace guest an appropriate greeting.

He thrived on the chase, lived for the challenge in all aspects of his life and at times yearned for a respite from his mission of revenge. Erotic fantasy was his specialty, sex his second calling. When he set his sights on a conquest, he ignored all obstacles that stood in the way of achieving his goal. Yet one goal he had never achieved…

Refusing to relive the regrets, Rayad decided the woman with the golden hair would be worth his best efforts to know her, if only for a brief time. If they decided they did not suit each other, so be it. Yet if they did, then the world was rife with possibilities, including a journey into pure pleasure…and a brief escape from the sins of his past.

Although the mountainous terrain qualified as breathtaking, and the majestic palace looming before her storybook-worthy, Sunny McAdams didn't have the presence of mind to appreciate the enchanting scenery. She sought only solace, a refuge in which to reclaim her courage and return to the woman she once had been.

A few months ago, she'd come to this obscure Middle Eastern country called Bajul to visit her beloved fraternal twin sister, Piper, who'd married a bona-fide Arabian prince. That day, she had been happy with life, secure in her job as a journalist and comfortably settled into a casual relationship with a really good guy. Two weeks later, everything had fallen apart. Now she felt terribly sad and a whole lot alone. Beaten down, but not broken. No one could ever break her, even those who had tried.

Yet for some reason, she felt as if someone might be watching her. Then again, her paranoia had grown by leaps and bounds since the kidnapping. Lately everyone appeared to be the enemy, from cab drivers to convenience-store workers.

As much as she hated to admit it, she needed family now, Piper in particular. Their personality differences had never interfered when it came to sensing each other's emotional needs. And that connection had led to her sister's invitation to visit for however long it took for Sunny to regroup.

As she stood by the car and waited for further instruction, she didn't possess enough energy to insist that she was quite capable of opening her own door and carrying her own luggage. *Luggage* was definitely an overstatement when describing the lone duffel bag and small carry-on case now in the hands of an attendant all decked out in white muslin. She'd learned to travel light and pack very little in the course of her work. Covering breaking news in some of the most obscure places on earth required only minimal supplies. At least today she'd exchanged the khakis and T-shirts for black slacks and a white, tailored, buttoned-up blouse, as dressed up as she'd been in quite a while.

When the driver gestured toward the entry, two

beefy guards opened the heavy, wooden double doors, allowing her access to the ornate Mehdi palace. And after she stepped inside, her footsteps echoed in the three-story foyer as she followed the man with her bag, passing several golden statuettes and exquisite artwork.

The attendant paused before the towering staircase, turned and set the duffel onto the polished stone floor near Sunny's feet. "If you will kindly wait here, I will summon your sister," he said, his tone thick with a Middle Eastern accent.

"Of course," she replied politely, although she wasn't sure why she had to wait. She couldn't imagine Piper had forgotten she was due to arrive at this hour. Then again, considering her sibling had stepped into the role of mother to the sheikh's infant son, she could have been detained by a wet diaper.

As the minutes ticked off, Sunny passed the time studying several portraits of regal-looking royals lining the stone walls, including the current king, the stoic and darkly handsome Rafiq Mehdi and his debonair brother, Zain. She then paused at the painting depicting the lighter-haired Adan, the youngest Mehdi son, and her new brother-in-law. She had to admit Piper had landed herself one good-looking pilot-prince, and the person who'd painted this picture had nailed every detail, right down to the guy's dimples.

After Sunny leaned over to better see the artist's signature, she immediately straightened from shock when she noted her twin's familiar handwriting. She then backtracked and checked every painting to find that Piper had created each and every one, and she'd done a darn good job. Finally, her sister had realized her overdue dream of becoming an artist. And she'd become a princess in the process. Amazing.

"Not too shabby at all," she muttered aloud. "It's about time you were wrested from our grandfather's clutches."

"Parental influences can be a challenge."

Sunny's hand automatically went to her throat as she spun around in search of the owner of the darkly masculine voice…and contacted the most intense near-black eyes she'd ever seen. He shouted military man from the top of his close-cropped black hair, to the bottom of his brown combat boots, yet his jaw was spattered with whiskers, as if he hadn't shaved in a while. The tan fatigues and black T-shirt pulled tight over his extremely toned chest, the short sleeves revealing standard-issue muscles that said he meant business, proved to be quite the distraction. So did his self-assured stance and the somewhat arrogant lift of his chin.

As he boldly assessed her from forehead to feet, Sunny's journalist's instinct kicked into overdrive, bringing with it a series of descriptors. Stealth. Mysterious. Sexy as hell.

The impact of the last thought caused heat to fan over her face and snake down her throat as the overwhelming need to escape took hold. She refused to give in to that urge.

When he didn't speak she offered her hand for a shake. "I'm Sunny McAdams. And you are?"

He stepped forward and enveloped her extended

hand in one very large palm. "Greatly pleased to meet you."

Two more words came to mind—practiced player. After he released his grasp, Sunny hugged her arms to her middle as if that somehow guarded her from the impact of his inescapable aura of power. "Do you have a name or should I try to guess?"

"Rayad," he replied without even hinting at a smile, but his gaze never faltered. Oh, no. He just kept staring at her as if trying to read her mind. Hopefully he couldn't, because she harbored too many secrets she would never reveal to a stranger.

Sunny inclined her head and studied him straight on, showing him she wasn't about to cower under his assessment. "Ah, a man of few words who apparently doesn't have a last name."

"You made it!"

She tore her attention from the stranger and brought it to her dark-haired, blue-eyed bubbly sister practically bounding down the stairs to the right. Before Piper reached the bottom landing, Sunny risked a glance to find that the mystifying Rayad was nowhere to be found.

As soon as Piper's feet hit the floor below the final step, she drew Sunny into a voracious hug. "I'm so glad you're here."

"So am I," she said after they ended the embrace. "And I can't tell you how much I appreciate you letting me hang out here for a while."

"You're welcome to stay as long as you like," Piper said as she surveyed Sunny's face. "You look terrible."

That could explain why Mystery Man had been staring at her nonstop. "Gee, thanks, sis. I didn't know the invitation came with insults."

Piper rolled her eyes to the gold-bedecked ceiling. "I meant you look exhausted. You couldn't look terrible if you tried."

Oh, but she did. She was well aware how badly her blond hair needed a trim and how pale she'd become since she'd left the field. "I'm in dire need of some sun and sleep, that's for sure. Spa treatments couldn't hurt."

Piper grinned. "Well, you've come to the right place. Or maybe I should say the right palace."

Sunny felt as if she'd been transported back to a better place and time, when she and her twin hadn't had a care in the world, in spite of the fact they hadn't had a caring mother. "Very funny, Pookie Bear."

Her sister scowled. "Please don't let my husband hear you call me that, Sunshine. He'll grab on to the nickname like a fish on a worm and won't let go."

"Tell you what," she said. "You can the *Sunshine* and I'll forget the *Pookie*."

"But your name is Sunshine."

"And you know how much I hate that."

"All right, it's a deal." Piper hooked her arm through Sunny's. "Now I shall escort you to your accommodations. For this visit, I've selected the first-floor guest quarters reserved for very special guests. Lots of privacy."

Unlike the last stay at the palace, this time Sunny needed privacy and a place to hide away, at least when she wasn't expected to socialize with the in-laws. "I only require a bed and a bath."

"Oh, you'll have both," Piper said as she led her down a lengthy corridor off the foyer. "And your own private garden."

"As long as I don't have to tend it, that sounds great."

After they navigated a narrow hallway flanked by more polished rock walls, Piper paused in front of a pair of gleaming wooden doors and opened them wide. "Enter this chamber fit for a princess. Or the princess's sister."

Sunny stepped over the threshold and visually searched the massive room, awed by the absolute grandeur, including an intricately carved headboard, red satin spread and a scattering of matching red and gold chairs. She turned to Piper and smiled. "Where's my tiara?"

"I'll have one sent up," she said. "Bathroom's to the right, complete with massive soaking tub and a car-wash-size shower, in case you want to have a party with a companion or ten."

She didn't even have one companion, let alone ten. When the image of the patently sexy, albeit elusive Rayad jumped into her brain, she mentally shoved it away. But she couldn't dispel the suffocating imagines of confinement at the hands of a criminal. She couldn't rid herself of the concern that she might never function as the normal sensual woman she'd once been. "Do you have a few minutes for a brief visit, or do you have to tend to royal duties or baby stuff?"

Piper plopped down onto a gold brocade divan.

"Sure. Sam won't be up from his nap for another half hour or so."

Sunny joined her on the less-than-comfortable sofa. "So how is my nephew these days?"

Her sister revealed a mother's smile. "He's fat and sassy and a very active eight-month-old. He started crawling fairly early, and now he's pulling up on furniture poised to take off on his chubby little legs at any time. But I really expect him to climb before he walks."

She expected Piper to burst at the seams with pride at any moment. "I assume the supermodel hasn't given you and Adan any trouble since the adoption."

"Not one bit. As far as everyone in the kingdom knows, Sam is my son."

Sunny took her sister's hand. "He is your son in every way that counts."

"You're right," Piper said. "And not only am I a mother, I have been commissioned as the official palace portrait artist. It's been a juggling act over the past few months, but I've had a lot of help with Sam from the staff and my gorgeous husband. I just finished Adan's painting two days ago and I hope it's up to speed."

Sunny smiled. "I saw the paintings, and Piper, they're beautiful. I'm so glad you tore yourself away from our grandfather's business so you could finally do what you've wanted to do for years."

Piper shrugged. "Believe me, if I hadn't met Adan, I'd probably still be acting as the company's goodwill ambassador. However, that position directly led to my husband."

Sunny grinned around an unexpected nip of envy.

"You must have shown him some mighty fine goodwill, among other things."

After they shared in a laugh, Piper's expression turned suddenly serious. "Enough about me. How are you doing?"

She'd been dreading this part of the visit—recounting the details of what led to her breakup with Cameron. Horrific details that she'd relived every day and night since the traumatic experience. "I'm doing much better than the last time we spoke. I've moved past the anger and on to acceptance." Though she would never quite accept her former lover's abandonment when she'd needed him most.

"It's not your fault," Piper said, as if she could read her thoughts. "He wasn't good enough for you if he couldn't face what happened."

"He tried, Piper. I was a mess."

"He didn't try hard enough, and that makes him a jerk."

"He was dealing with his own guilt for not following me that day so he could ride in and save me."

"Stop making excuses for him, Sunny. You were brutally attacked and abducted and that's not something anyone can get over in a matter of days. If I'd been through the same thing, I know Adan would have stuck by me."

Something suddenly occurred to her. "You haven't mentioned the attack to Adan, have you?"

Piper shook her head. "No. He thinks you're here because of the breakup. I don't like keeping things from him, but I did promise you I wouldn't say anything."

She'd known she could count on her sister for discretion. "Thank you. The network decided to keep it under wraps."

Piper frowned. "Why? Are they afraid you're going to sue them?"

"No. They're respecting my privacy. They know if word gets out, I'll be headline news instead of covering it." She sighed. "I keep trying to tell myself we knew what we were walking into. What we'd been walking into for the past three years. Greed breeds criminals, but you never really know who they are until you meet up with one on a dark street. And in one moment of carelessness, your whole perspective on life changes when facing possible death."

Piper leaned over and hugged her. "I hope you're going to consider staying in the States when you resume your career."

She had considered it, then nixed that idea altogether, a fact she chose to withhold from her twin for the time being. "That's going to be up to the network, provided they even want me after I've been on leave for two months."

"The network adores you, Sunny. I'm sure they'll welcome you back with open arms. Do you still have your apartment in Atlanta?"

Sunny shook her head. "Nana convinced me to give it up when my lease ran out while I was staying with her and Poppa. My things are in storage in Charleston."

"Well, you can always live in the guesthouse permanently since I've vacated the premises."

She'd rather eat collard greens. "A little bit of the

grandparents goes a long way. If I decided to work solely in the U.S., I'd move back to Atlanta."

Piper gave her another quick hug. "I hope you do. I wouldn't have to worry about you fending off poisonous snakes in some rain forest."

At least she hadn't brought up unseen attackers. "You could have gone all year without mentioning those foul creatures," she said, followed by a yawn.

Piper came to her feet and smiled. "You apparently have a lot of catch-up to do on your sleep. So feel free to take a long nap."

If only it were that simple. Sleep hadn't come easily, at least nightmare-free sleep. "That sounds good, but it's not that long until bedtime."

"True, but don't hesitate to try the giant bathtub before dinner," Piper added.

Sunny stood and stretched her arms above her head. "Speaking of dinner, who'll be joining us for the evening meal?"

"Everyone," Piper said. "My husband, of course. Zain and Madison and their toddlers since they've recently returned from Los Angeles. King Rafiq and an extremely pregnant Queen Maysa. Oh, and a cousin, Rayad Rostam, who showed up two days ago."

Finally, Mystery Man was no longer quite the mystery. "Since his last name isn't Mehdi, how is he related?"

"His father and the former queen were siblings, I think, but I don't know much more. I haven't had the opportunity to speak with my husband for three whole days, thanks to some top-secret training mission where

he flies planes at warp speed. But I'll be sure to introduce you to Rayad tonight, and you can interview him."

"I met him," Sunny blurted without thought. "While I was waiting for you in the foyer. But he didn't say much more than a few words."

Piper's smile arrived full-force. "He's gorgeous, isn't he?"

Unfortunately. "I didn't notice, and you're not supposed to notice since you're now a married woman."

"But I'm not blind, and neither are you."

Her twin knew her all too well. "Fine, he's gorgeous. Satisfied?"

Piper's expression said she wasn't. "Maybe you should get to know him while you're here. It's my understanding he is presently unattached."

Sunny held up both hands, palms forward. "Stop right there. I'm not in the market for a man, if that's what you're thinking."

"I'm thinking you could use a diversion after the idiot left you high and dry."

"It's too soon, Piper. Cameron and I haven't been apart that long." And her internal wounds resulting from the attack had yet to heal. Wounds she had yet to reveal to her twin.

"And by your own admission, Sunny, you loved Cameron, but you weren't *in love* with him."

She'd argued those points with herself, but that hadn't eased the hurt. "Color me gun-shy."

Piper's features softened into a sympathetic look. "Maybe it's time you make a sincere effort to rejoin the land of the living, Sunny. I'm not suggesting you sleep with Rayad. I'm suggesting you use your skills to find out what he's all about and leave all options open. A challenge of sorts to get your mind off your troubles. And lucky for you, he's staying in the room right next door."

She found that somewhat odd, and a little disconcerting. "Doesn't he have a house of his own?"

"Since he's undoubtedly rich as sin like the rest of the family, I assume he does. But Maysa told me that Rafiq insisted he stay here while he's recovering from an injury he sustained during some kind of incident."

He'd looked perfectly healthy to Sunny. Very healthy. "What did he injure?"

Her sister grinned. "I'm not sure. Why don't you ask him? Better still, why don't you request he show you?"

"Not interested," she said, worried that she might never be able to experience true intimacy again. "Besides, I've never really been drawn to the strong, macho, silent type."

Piper barked out a laugh on her way to the door. "Yeah, right, Sunshine. Aside from Cameron, that's the only type that's ever held your interest."

Bristling from the truth, Sunny trailed behind her sister and prepared for a debate. "Don't you dare do anything stupid like try to fix me up, Pookie."

Piper spun around and scowled. "You promised you wouldn't call me that."

"You promised, too."

"Okay, you're right. No more Pookie or Sunshine."

"It's a deal."

"And I also promise not to play cupid," Piper continued, "although Madison tells me Rayad's a really nice guy if you can get past all that machismo. Just something to consider between now and the evening meal."

After Piper closed the door behind her, Sunny perched on the edge of the mattress and toed out of her flats. She'd already surmised Rayad Rostam was a testosterone-ridden military man, and that should be all she needed to know. Yet her innate inquisitiveness urged her to learn more about him. She craved peeling back those personality layers to reveal the man behind the steely persona. She truly needed to investigate him further, from a solely journalistic standpoint, of course. Even if she proved to be drawn to him on a physical level, a virile man like Rayad wouldn't want the closed-off, fearful woman she'd become. Not even a nice guy could handle that—case in point, her former lover, Cameron.

Rayad Rostam a nice guy? She frankly had her doubts about that.

Two

Macho Man had a squirming toddler in his lap, and he didn't seem to mind.

Seated across from Rayad Rostam at the lengthy dining table, for the past ten minutes Sunny had witnessed his remarkable patience with brown-haired, chatty, two-year-old Cala, daughter of the former playboy prince, Zain Mehdi, and his wife, Madison, the resident palace fixer of all things scandalous. The patient sheikh didn't seem concerned that the little girl had dotted his T-shirt with cheese cracker remnants. He didn't appear to care when she poked at his mouth, as if it held some sort of magic. Sunny suspected it probably did. The tolerant sheikh simply kept his lips sealed against the intrusion and gently extracted her hand from his face, followed by a kiss on her palm.

She certainly couldn't fault a guy who apparently had an affinity for children. She also hadn't been able to ignore the furtive glances he'd tossed her way during dinner, even though the to-die-for skewered chicken, tasty cheese and hummus side dish should have earned all her attention. Fortunately, no one else seemed to notice, thanks to the ongoing adult conversation and occasional screech from an overstimulated infant, namely her nephew, Sam.

When Cala wriggled from Rayad's lap, Sunny noticed discomfort pass over his face as his hand went to his upper right side. The wound Piper mentioned apparently involved his rib cage. Another mystery solved, several more to go, including the hint of sadness in his eyes as Cala turned and waved to him before claiming a spot in her father's lap.

But at the moment, the effects of jet lag had Sunny considering putting off her sheikh fact-finding mission until a later date. And when the queen and king rose from their chairs and excused themselves, followed by Zain and Madison and their twins, she saw that as an excuse to make her escape.

Sunny tossed her napkin aside, came to her feet and regarded Piper, who was seated next to the silent Rayad. "Dinner was great," she began, "but I really need to retire before I nod off in the dessert plate."

Piper stood and removed Sam from his highchair then turned him around to face Sunny. "Tell your auntie good-night, sweetie." The baby responded by flailing his arms around and making motoring noises.

"A chip off the old pilot block," Adan said, displaying

a dimpled grin as he stood with Rayad following suit. "I do hope you find your quarters satisfactory, Sunny."

"They're more than satisfactory," she replied as she rounded the table to kiss her nephew good-night, very aware that Rayad visually followed her movements. "I'm sure I'll sleep well as soon as I take my nightly walk. Any suggestions where I should do that?"

Adan nodded to the open dining room doors. "After you exit, take a right, and you'll find the entry to the courtyard."

"But be careful," Piper cautioned. "The grounds are like a maze. You might want to grab some bread crumbs and leave a trail, just in case."

"I have a fairly good sense of direction, so no worries."

After giving her twin a hug, and bidding everyone good-night, Sunny left the room and immediately located the doors leading to the expansive garden. She followed the labyrinth of stone walkways using the three-quarter moon as her guide, occasionally glancing behind her to keep the palace within her sights. When the path ended at a low retaining wall, she paused to study the twinkling lights dotting the valley below. A warm November breeze ruffled her hair, bringing with it the scent of exotic flowers. Back home the weather would be much cooler, and much of the fragrant foliage gone until spring. But not in this region. Most days brought pleasant weather, according to her hosts, yet rain had been forecasted in the next couple of days.

Feeling surprisingly serene, she looked up at the night sky to study the host of diamond-like stars. She welcomed the sense of peace she experienced for the first time in quite some time…

"Have you lost your way?"

For the second time that day, Sunny's heart vaulted into her throat. She spun around to face the familiar man standing in the shadows behind her. "I'm not lost, and do you have some bizarre need to scare me to death?"

"No. I was simply concerned for your well-being."

"Look, Mr.…Sheikh… What exactly is your official title?"

He took a step toward her, his handsome face only partially revealed in the limited light. "You may call me Rayad."

She'd like to call him a few unflattering names at the moment, and she would if he wasn't so darn intimidating—in an overtly male sort of way. "Look, Rayad, I have traveled to some of the most remote places in the world and navigated some of the most treacherous terrain. I can handle a palace garden."

"A garden that has been known to house deadly insects and asps."

Just when her heart had returned to its rightful place, he'd mentioned her biggest fear. Correction. Second biggest fear, if the truth were known. "Really? Snakes?"

"Yes."

She refused to let him see her uneasiness. "Would that be the reptile or human variety?"

"I have not personally encountered either in this garden," he said without even a touch of lightness in his tone. "However, I have been conditioned to protect women. Therefore, I feel it is necessary to ensure your safe return."

Her perfect opportunity to get to know him, but then he went and ruined it with the whole he-man posturing. Now she was determined to make a hasty escape and prove she could make it back to safety on her own. She had survived much, much worse. "Not all women need protection, Sheikh Rostam. Have a nice night."

After Sunny brushed past him, she paused to survey four directional options, crossed her fingers and chose the path to her right.

"You are going the wrong way."

Somewhat annoyed by his interference, and her irritating female reaction to the sexy timbre of his voice, she reluctantly faced him again. "I'm sure every way eventually leads back to the palace."

He moved closer. "Not necessarily. If you continue on your current course, you will reach the road leading to the village. And if not careful, you could tumble down the cliff if you lose your footing."

Wasn't he just the bearer of good news? If she refused his offer, she could be allowing pride to overrule safety, a mistake she'd already made that had brought about severe consequences. If she accepted his aid, she could find out what made him tick, and avoid falling to her death. Option two sounded the most favorable, although not completely without risk. "Fine. Lead the way."

After Rayad chose the trail heading in the opposite direction, Sunny came to his side and kept her focus straight ahead. And as they walked a few yards in silence, she mentally dashed through a list of subtle questions, choosing the most logical query to begin her impromptu interview. "Piper mentioned you'd recently suffered an injury during military training."

"Broken ribs."

"Did you run into something?"

"A fist."

Definitely a man of few words, or two words, as the case might be. "Must've been some tough hand-to-hand combat. Is training troops primarily your duty?"

"No. Intelligence."

Figured. "So you're a spy guy, huh?"

"In a manner of speaking."

"I bet you have a code name like Scorpion, or perhaps Snake."

"That information is classified."

She wondered if he ever let down his guard, or smiled, for that matter. "How long have you been serving?"

"Twelve years. I entered the military at the age of twenty-one."

Progress. She now knew his age and that he was only six years her senior. Not too bad. Not that their age difference should matter one iota. "Are you married?" Now why had she asked that when she already knew the answer?

"No, I am not."

"Have you ever been married?"

His long hesitation was a bit telling, or maybe she was reading too much into it. Then it suddenly dawned on her that he might think she was interested in him.

Time to set the record straight. "I ask because I've known quite a few military men who find it difficult to maintain a marriage. Understandably so when they're away much of the time. And I can relate with my line of work. Covering global news isn't conducive to having a serious relationship."

He paused, reached down to his right, snapped a plumeria from one grouping and offered it to her. "Have you been wed?" he asked as they continued on.

Both the question and the gesture caught her off guard. "Thanks, and I've never been married."

"Are you currently involved with anyone?"

Somehow the interviewer had become the interviewee. "I was involved briefly with a colleague, but that's been over for a while now."

"The man who apparently drove you to seek out your sister."

He presented the comment as a statement, not a question, leading Sunny to believe he knew much more about her than she knew about him. "You're right in a manner of speaking. How did you learn that?"

"Rafiq mentioned this to me when I inquired about you."

She'd expected her sister had been the messenger, not the king. "What else did he say?"

"He warned me to stay away from you."

One more shock in a series of several. "Seriously? Does he think I have the plague or homicidal intent aimed at men?"

He almost cracked a smile. "Do you?"

"No, I do not, and I have a hard time believing Rafiq believes that, either."

A slight span of silence passed before he spoke again. "The king believes you are too great a temptation for a man such as myself."

"Oh, I see." And she did, very clearly, even if his expression remained unreadable. "He thinks that if you attempt to seduce me, I'd be too vulnerable to resist. Clearly, he doesn't know me at all." Or at least the woman she used to be.

"Perhaps that is what he believes, but I do not view you as a vulnerable woman."

The compliment and the flower earned him a few points, even though she did inexplicably feel somewhat defenseless around him. His mystery and aura of power threw her mentally off-kilter. "I'm happy we've established I'm not some simpering Southern belle who needs saving."

"I do not understand the term *Southern belle*, but I do believe you are a highly sensual woman."

She loosened the chokehold she had on the poor plumeria. "What brought you to that conclusion?"

He slipped his hands in the pockets of his slacks and failed to look directly at her. "You are passionate about your work. You have put yourself in danger many times for the sake of your career."

She forced away the sudden terrifying images, with great effort. "Rafiq told you details about my occupation, too?"

"No. I perused your network's website."

She should probably be a bit wary that he'd conducted an internet search, but she was actually curious. "What prompted you to look me up?"

He sent her a fast glance, giving her a drive-by view of his damnable dark eyes. "When we spoke in the foyer today, I was intrigued by you."

She couldn't fault him since she'd felt the same about him. "Maybe I should search the net so I can learn more about you."

"You will find nothing."

Apparently he worked deep undercover, or he could be attempting to divert her from discovering information he preferred she not know. "In that case, tell me about yourself. The man, not the soldier."

He streaked a palm over the back of his neck. "I am the only child of a sultan who resides in Dubai with my mother."

"Considering how well you handled Cala tonight, are you sure you don't have a secret baby hidden away like your cousin, Adan?"

As he glanced her way, some unnamed emotion reflected from his eyes then disappeared as quickly as it had come. "I have no children."

"Then you have a gift."

He continued to focus on the path and not her. "Children are a gift. Too often they are used as pawns during war."

He'd probably witnessed unspeakable acts in his tenure as a soldier. That could explain why he'd seemed so sullen after Cala returned to Zain. She did find it odd that with his royal lineage, he would choose the military as his occupation and serve a country that obviously wasn't his homeland. "How did you end up in Bajul?"

"Adan and I attended the same military academy in the United Kingdom, though I was three years ahead of him. After I graduated, he encouraged me to consider joining him in the armed forces. My father gave his blessing, as well."

"You evidently didn't pick up the British-speak like Adan. In fact, you don't really have an accent at all, and your English is perfect."

"I am required to know many languages."

"How many?"

"Ten."

Incredible. "Do you fly jets, too?"

He shook his head. "No. I am strictly involved in ground forces."

She lifted the flower to her nose and drew in the wonderful scent. "If I were in the military and had my choice, I'd definitely learn to fly. Piper, on the other hand, hates planes. Ironic that she would marry a pilot."

"Reason is not always present when human emotion is involved."

How well she knew that. "Since I'm positive you can't be all work and no play, do you have any hobbies? Any interests beyond your job?"

"I have a weakness for beautiful women such as yourself."

Had she'd known she'd walk right into the typical playboy trap, she wouldn't have asked. "You don't get out much, do you?"

"Do not question my ability to recognize beauty," he said. "However, I do find humility very attractive."

False flattery would get him nowhere, especially since she hadn't felt attractive in quite some time. "I personally find arrogance off-putting."

Finally, he smiled—a small one—but a smile all the same. "Do you believe me to be arrogant?"

"I believe you're the kind of man who uses compliments to your advantage."

As they neared the palace entrance, Rayad paused beneath one of the lights lining the walkway, giving Sunny a good look at his handsome features, particularly his expressive eyes. "I am simply a man who speaks the truth," he said.

She hugged her arms to her middle, the flower wilting in her grasp. "Would that be all the time or only when it's convenient?"

"I am forced to withhold some information for security reasons. Yet when it comes to my attraction to a woman, I have nothing to hide, and I find I am extremely attracted to you."

She suspected many a woman had willingly given him anything he'd requested with only the crook of his finger and a come-hither look. She had no intention of doing that for many reasons. "Please explain to me how you could even remotely find me attractive after knowing me such a short time."

"Attraction is at times immediate, and oftentimes without explanation."

She couldn't exactly argue since she had to admit she found him illogically attractive, as well. And that in itself could be dangerous. "You're referring to *physical* attraction."

"That is the bait that encourages two people to explore the possibilities."

As Rayad studied her face, his gaze coming to rest on her mouth before trekking back to her eyes, she could imagine several possibilities. Tempting possibilities. Inadvisable and unattainable possibilities in light of her recent past.

Forcing herself back into reality, Sunny pointed the posy at the double doors. "Since it's getting fairly late, we should probably call it a night. Sleep well."

He inclined his head and narrowed his eyes. "Do you sleep well, or do nightmares plague you?"

Her entire body tensed with the fear he knew more about her than she'd first assumed. "Why would you believe I have nightmares?"

He leaned back against the stone ledge behind him and folded his arms across his broad chest. "I know you have seen carnage in your line of work. And with that carnage comes images that haunt you in dark and daylight."

Somewhat relieved he evidently didn't know everything, she wanted desperately to deny his accurate assumption. But she sensed he possessed an expert ranking when it came to character study, and therefore chose a partial lie. "I've had a few bad dreams, but it's not an every-night occurrence."

"Then you are fortunate," he said.

She took a step toward him in an effort to better read his reaction. "I take it you speak from experience."

He lifted his shoulders slightly in a shrug. "I am not immune to dreams that disturb my sleep."

"Then you've seen your share of horrors."

"Many in the past, and I expect more in the future."

Sheer curiosity to dissect this enigmatic man drew her to his side. "At the risk of sounding idealistic and illogical, I don't understand why the world has to be that way."

"Evil," he said, a strong cast of anger in his tone. "I have seen unspeakable acts forced on innocents by those with no conscience."

"So have I." She had been the victim of that very thing, though she refused to see herself as a victim. "It has made me rethink my career choice. I'm considering returning to the States when I go back to work."

"You will never be happy."

She faced him, leaned a hip against the wall and rested her elbow atop the ledge. "You're very bold to make that presumption."

Finally, he turned toward her and made eye contact. "I know your kind. You live for adventure and the thrill of chasing the story. You said in your biography you choose to ignore danger to seek the truth."

Damn the internet. "Yes, I did, but I'm not sure I feel that way anymore."

He gave her a look of surprise laced with suspicion. "Has something happened to change your attitude?"

The question had hit too close to home. If not careful, she might start confessing. "Burnout, I guess you could say. And it's definitely time for me to retire. If I'm lucky, this little jaunt through the snake-ridden garden has tired me out enough to drift off fairly quickly. Thanks so much for the companionship. I truly enjoyed it."

When Sunny turned and started away, he quickly clasped her hand. The sudden action caused her to wrest away and turn toward him, a knee-jerk reaction she'd developed since the attack.

"I do not wish to harm you," he said in a tempered tone.

She shivered slightly. "I know, and I apologize for my jumpiness. Just a little fallout due to the job. I've learned to always be on guard."

He pushed off the wall and approached her, leaving a scant few inches between them when he stopped. Then without warning, he reached out and pushed a tendril of hair from her cheek. "I find you very captivating, Sunny McAdams, and I hope I have the pleasure of speaking with you at length again."

"That's definitely a possibility," she said then hooked a thumb over her shoulder. "But if I don't get some rest, the next time you see me I might be babbling like a mad woman."

He smiled again. A fully formed smile that lessened the intensity in his eyes, but not his appeal. Not in the least. "Should you require assistance during the night, I am residing in the room next to yours."

That fact certainly wouldn't do a darn thing for her insomnia. "Thank you, but I'll be fine. I'm sure I'll see you tomorrow."

"That would be my pleasure."

The way he'd said *pleasure*—in a deep, sensual

tone—prompted some fairly sexual images in Sunny's muddled mind. And long after she left Rayad to settle into bed, she allowed them to fully form—only to have horrendous memories interrupt the welcome bliss.

She wondered if she would ever move past her fears and resume a normal life. If she would ever forget the harrowing experience. If she would ever be able to trust a man again.

For some reason, she truly wanted to trust Rayad Rostam, but she wasn't certain she could.

Three

He had never met a woman who recoiled at an innocent touch…until tonight. Rayad had pondered Sunny's reaction as he stripped off all of his clothing and stretched out on his back on the bed, naked.

He had wanted to kiss her and would have attempted it if not for her response. She had not necessarily been repulsed, but she had been afraid. He suspected that fear stemmed from a recent experience. He had seen it in her eyes, heard the wariness in her voice when he had asked about her decision to return home. Unless he knew the cause of her fear, he could only speculate. Yet he truly believed Sunny would not be forthcoming with that information. In that regard, she was very much like him, withholding details due to a lack of trust. However, one person would mostly hold the answers he sought.

Though he should wait until morning to question Piper, Rayad's thirst for the truth drove him from the bed. He retrieved a guest robe from the closet and slipped it on before entering the hallway. He strode through the corridors and sprinted up the staircase to the living quarters. Once there, he paused and attempted to discern which room belonged to Adan and his new bride. Fortunately, a meek-looking, dark-haired woman walked out one door to his immediate right and met his gaze, obviously surprised to find a nearly-naked man standing in the hallway.

After recognition dawned in her expression, she bowed her head slightly and muttered, "Your Highness."

He tightened the sash on the gaping robe. "I need to locate Sheikh Adan's room."

"At the end of the hall," she said, keeping her eyes averted as she pointed to her right. "But they do not wish to be disturbed. That is why I am tending to the young prince tonight."

If he retained any decorum whatsoever, he would take his leave. This mission was too important. "I will make certain you are not held responsible for the disturbance."

With that, he headed to the designated quarters without glancing back. Once there, he rapped twice on the wooden surface and waited. He had almost given up when the door creaked open to reveal his disheveled cousin, also dressed in a robe. "Bloody hell, Rayad," Adan muttered. "I hope you tell me we've gone to war, the only excuse I will accept for you showing up here in the middle of the night."

"There is no war, but I must speak to your wife."

"*My* wife is not presentable at the moment, and why would you need to speak to her?"

"I need to inquire about her sister."

Adan narrowed his eyes. "If you are entertaining thoughts of garnering permission to seduce Sunny, discard them now. She does not need to have you hounding her under the circumstances."

Perhaps he could bypass Piper after all. "Which circumstances would those be?"

"She was thrown over by some bastard and has suffered a severe broken heart. Those were my wife's exact words."

Siblings had been known to withhold truths from one another before, as it had been often with his cousins Adan and Zain. Or perhaps in this matter a wife was withholding information from her spouse. "And you are certain Piper is not concealing other details pertaining to her sister?"

He presented a stern scowl. "I have no reason not to believe what she told me. Now what is this all about?"

"I sensed there is more to Sunny's sabbatical than the end of a relationship when I was with her this evening."

Adan took on a murderous expression. "Define *when I was with her*."

"We took a walk together in the garden."

"And where, Rayad, did you end your walk?"

He realized exactly what his cousin was implying. "We ended the walk in the garden, and that is when I realized she has unexplained fears."

"Of what? You?"

"Indirectly, yes. When I attempted to touch her—"

"*Where* did you attempt to touch her?"

"Her hand."

"Are you bloody sure you didn't reach a bit higher than that?"

Adan's question echoed loudly through the hallway and apparently disturbed his bride, who suddenly appeared in the doorway. "If you two don't lower your voices, you're going to wake the entire palace, including our son and the twins. What in heaven's name has you both so worked up?"

Adan pointed at Rayad. "This cad made a pass at your sister."

His wife seemed surprisingly calm. "She's an attractive woman, honey."

Rayad felt the need to defend his honor. "I only attempted to take her hand, yet her reaction to that innocent gesture has led me to believe she has possibly suffered a recent trauma."

"I told him it was a traumatic breakup," Adan said. "With the soundman."

Piper frowned at her husband. "He's a cameraman, Adan, and what kind of reaction are you referring to?"

"She startles easily," Rayad answered. "It is as if she is fearful of many things."

Piper's gaze briefly faltered. "That's understandable considering she throws herself into some fairly precarious situations due to her job."

Her lack of eye contact, coupled with the slight tremor in her voice, served to support Rayad's suspicions. "I have seen this behavior before in those who have experienced violence in some manner. It can be indicative of post traumatic stress disorder."

Adan raised a brow. "It is probably indicative of your penchant for making unwanted advances on an unsuspecting woman."

He despised having his honor questioned. "I never force myself on unwitting women, Adan. And you have no cause to make accusations. At one time you were much worse in regard to making advances."

Adan took obvious offense over the affront. "I have always been noble when it comes to the fairer sex, cousin."

Patience waning, Rayad glared at him. "As have I, *cousin.*"

"Rayad's right," Piper interjected, drawing both their attention.

Adan regarded his wife with a confused expression. "Forgive me, Piper, but you haven't known Rayad long enough to make that character judgment."

She shook her head. "He's right about Sunny. Something did happen to her a couple of months ago."

"Why did you not tell me this before now?" Adan asked.

"Because she made me promise not to say anything," she replied. "But frankly, I'm worried about her. Even more so now." She both looked and sounded extremely concerned.

Exactly as he'd predicted. Rayad now needed all the details Sunny's sibling could give him. "What precisely happened to her?"

"She was in a small village in Angola," Piper said.

"Late one night she went for a walk on the streets. She was ambushed and attacked by some unknown assailants. They held her captive for a few hours before she managed to get away."

"Was she sexually assaulted?" Adan asked before Rayad had the opportunity.

"No," Piper stated adamantly. "She was very clear about that. Thankfully, nothing was broken aside from her spirits, but it did take a while for her to recover, according to her. In my opinion, she still hasn't."

Two questions weighed heavily on his mind—why had her former lover not sought her out, and had anyone been held accountable? "Did they apprehend the assailants?"

"They never did," she said. "Sunny told me a lot of people travel there to mine for diamonds, so it could have been anyone from anywhere in the world. She doesn't expect to ever find out the identity of the responsible parties."

How well he knew that concept, yet he refused to accept that conclusion. He had lived with his own mystery for many years, and lived his life for revenge. "Thank you for providing this information, Piper. It does explain her behavior. And now I know how I should handle the situation."

"Leave her be, Rayad," Adan demanded. "She's come here to be alone and heal her wounds."

His cousin's cautions would not deter him from his goal. "And she cannot tend to that herself. I can provide the support she needs during her visit here in Bajul."

"It's your idea of support that concerns me," Adan said.

"Maybe Rayad's help is exactly what Sunny needs," Piper interjected. "She's not going to listen to me. If he can get through to her, he has my blessing."

Adan pointed at him. "Do not do anything inadvisable, Rayad."

He nodded his acknowledgment. "I will handle the situation with the greatest of care."

And he would, despite his desire for the beautiful, troubled Sunny McAdams. Perhaps this would be his chance to engage in an honorable endeavor. An opportunity to prove he had not completely lost his soul. Perhaps he could save this woman where before he had failed another. Perhaps he could prove to himself that he was a man worthy of salvation—not the soldier who had no hope for redemption.

"Wake up, sleepyhead."

Frightened and disoriented, Sunny jolted her head up from the pillow and attempted to focus on the figure before her. Thankfully, the familiar face and smile helped calm her raw nerves and bring her back into reality. Not that she was overly happy with her sister's sudden appearance, nor did she understand why she had her arms full of garment bags.

Sunny threw back the covers, climbed out of the too-tall bed and sighed. "You could've knocked, Piper."

"I did. Twice, in fact. And I'm really sorry if I scared you."

"I'm not scared." The slight tremor in her voice belied her confidence.

"It's okay, Sunny. I know it's been tough to overcome the effects of your ordeal."

Her twin couldn't even imagine what she'd been through. "What time is it, and did you raid the local dry cleaners?"

Piper looked down at the bags as if she didn't remember what she had clutched in her arms. "It's close to noon, and no, I did not raid the dry cleaners. I did, however, raid the local boutique earlier this morning to find you something suitable to wear."

Lovely. Just what she needed after a restless night— wardrobe criticism. "You told me to pack what I normally pack."

"Yes, but tonight we'll be attending an event that requires something a bit more formal than cotton and khakis."

Sunny swept her mussed hair back with one hand and adjusted the top of her sleep shirt to better cover her neck. "What event?"

Clearly bent on avoiding the question, Piper laid the bags across the end of the bed and unzipped the first of three garment bags. "This is my personal favorite," she said as she withdrew a black, slinky dress.

The plunging neckline would never work, not when she needed to hide the reminders of her recent torment. "Too much bling, and you still didn't answer my question."

Piper tightened the band securing her dark auburn hair into a low ponytail before smoothing a palm down her flowing peach-colored sundress. "It's no big deal, really. Just a simple state dinner Madison arranged several months ago. A few dignitaries hoping to hold court with the king. Some schmoozing. That kind of thing."

The kind of thing that made her head hurt. "Am I required to attend?"

"No, but you'll miss a lot of great food." Piper withdrew another dress and held it up. "What about this one?"

She eyed the satin evening gown that reminded her of a shiny hothouse tomato. "You know I look horrible in red, and I've had fancy food before. Just bring me a take-out box after you're finished schmoozing. Or I'll scrounge around in the kitchen after the festivities if I get hungry."

"You can come to the banquet and leave early if you'd like." Piper brought out the final evening wear selection. "I'm sure Rayad wouldn't mind seeing you in this one."

"That's perfect." Sunny was caught off guard by the verbal seal of approval that spilled out of her mouth without thought. One mention of the mysterious sheikh, and she was ready to party. What in the heck was wrong with her? "I meant it would work if I decide to go, and it really is immaterial to me whether Rayad is there or not."

Her sister sighed like she'd lost her best gal pal. "Stop being so stubborn, Sunny. You need to get out and socialize a while. Meet new people. Get to know those you've already met, better."

She needed to stay in and lick her wounds. "Believe me, I had enough socializing to last a lifetime in my youth. I swore at our debutante ball I'd never put on another ball gown again."

Piper chuckled. "I remember how much you hated being a deb."

"And I remember how much you loved the attention, although I don't know why. That has to be the most antiquated tradition in the history of womankind."

Her sister's blue eyes sparkled with amusement. "It was worth it seeing you in that hoop skirt. Now promise you'll attend tonight or I'll post pictures of that on the web."

Sunny snatched the gown from Piper's clutches. "Fine. I'll put on the darn dress and parade around for fifteen minutes, thirty tops."

Piper frowned. "Funny, I thought this royal blue one would be your least favorite. And I know how much you detest a high neck."

Not when she had an obvious scar to hide. She didn't dare let her sister see the wound for fear she would have to explain, and she wasn't prepared to reveal the details yet, if ever. "I like the overall cut of the dress. Sleeveless, satin and simple, yet elegant."

"And also loose fitting," Piper said. "You won't be able to show off your figure that I've envied since we were teenagers."

She didn't care one whit how it looked on her. Much. She admittedly yearned to catch a glimpse of Rayad, and maybe continue her interview. "It's fine, Piper, and I've envied your curves for years. And that you got the blue eyes and I got stuck with green. Besides, I'm sure no one will notice me at all."

Piper barked out a laugh. "Sure, Sunny. Just keep telling yourself that. I'm fairly certain I know at least one man who'll be staring at you all evening, just like he did at dinner last night."

Darn if her sister hadn't noticed. "I have no clue what you're talking about."

"Rayad. He eyed you like you were dessert."

"He did not."

"Did so."

Sunny was simply too sleep-deprived to get into this now. "Go take care of your son."

"Aren't you going to try it on?" Piper asked, followed by her patent scowl.

Only after she was assured she had complete privacy. "I need to shower first, but I'm positive it will fit."

"We have yet to discuss your shoes."

Obviously her twin was intent on playing dress-up. "I have shoes."

"Heels?"

"What does it matter? The gown is floor-length so no one will see my feet anyway. And I promise not to wear sneakers or hiking boots."

"Or you could wear these." Piper reached into the pocket of one garment bag to retrieve a pair of silver sandals with three-inch heels. "The perfect finishing touch, and they'll give you a little height, although at five-six you really don't need that."

Her sister's long-time height envy was now showing. Sunny snatched the platform torture shoes and set them at the foot of the bed. "Great. I'm all set. Now if you don't mind, I need to bathe."

Piper gathered the remaining dresses into her arms and sighed. "If you're hungry, the chef has some lunch

for you in the kitchen. Wear a little extra makeup tonight, and if you need your hair done, Kira is a master."

She'd only briefly met the palace staffer and frankly
didn't trust anyone with her hair. "I can handle my hair,
so if you're done giving me orders, you can run along
now."

Piper backed toward the door, grinning. "You are so
going to totally blow Rayad away."

Her sister quickly left the room before Sunny could
insist she didn't need to impress anyone, let alone a man
who was virtually a stranger. She did need to get on
with the day and ignore thoughts of that man that had
played on her mind much of last night.

After making the bed, she made quick work of her
routine and emerged from the shower feeling somewhat more human. Then she caught sight of the raised
horizontal welt right above her collarbone and cringed.
They'd told her she could eventually have a plastic sur-
geon repair it, but in time she hoped to be brave enough
to wear it as a badge of honor. A reminder that life
could end on a moment's notice with one flick of a
switchblade.

Pushing the recollections aside, she dressed in a light
blue T-shirt that concealed the evidence, put on a pair
of white cotton shorts and slipped her feet into plain
beige flip-flops. Next step—finding food.

After twisting her damp hair into a knot at her nape,
Sunny walked out the door and strode down the lengthy
corridor, all the while considering the sinfully sexy
sheikh…until she realized she had no idea where she
was going when she hit a dead end in the hallway. She

could turn right or left, and decided on right, only to discover Rayad heading her way, as if she'd somehow conjured him up.

He continued to walk as he focused on a document in his hand, giving her a prime opportunity to covertly check him out. From the confident gait to the broad chest and all points up and down, he would be the kind of man worthy of a magical love spell. The kind of man who drew attention the moment he entered the room, or a confusing corridor in this instance. Then she remembered how she looked at the moment—wet-headed and bare-faced—and heat flowed over her cheeks, most likely leaving crimson in its wake.

Who cared if she wasn't dressed like a prom queen? So what if her appearance was barely fit for public viewing? It truly didn't matter what he thought. She didn't give a rat's patoot if he caught sight of her, turned and ran away.

Yet when he looked up and met her gaze, he continued to move toward her, a hint of a smile curling the corners of his sexy mouth. As the space disappeared between them, he stopped and tucked the papers under one arm. "Good afternoon, Sunny."

The sound of her name on his lips made her think about warm desert breezes, the whisper of his voice in her ear, making love at midnight beneath the stars…

Heaven help her, she had died and gone to Southern belle hell, where romantic ideals were as common as mint juleps.

She managed to clear her throat, but she couldn't quite clear her mind of the silly notion that he would ride in and save the day, complete with a sword and horse. "Good afternoon to you, too, Rayad. And before you ask, yes, I'm lost. Which way to the kitchen?"

He pointed behind him. "Maintain your current course and take a left immediately before the staircase, then follow the scent."

The only scent she discerned at the moment was him. An earthy, exotic scent that gave the flower the night before a run for its money. "I take it you've already had lunch."

"Yes, and breakfast several hours ago."

He probably thought she was an absolute slug. "I slept in."

"Apparently, yet this is a good thing. Did you rest well?"

As well as anyone plagued by visions of masked villains. "Fairly well. And you?"

"Not as much rest as I perhaps should, but I require little sleep."

"Oh." Now what? Ask him about his reading material? What he had planned for the day? Could she come along for the ride? Ride as in... "I guess I'll go grab something to eat."

No sooner than she'd said it when a silver-haired, golden-skinned gentleman dressed in white muslin came toward them at a fast clip, a tray balanced in one hand. Sunny stepped to one side to get out of his way, but he paused and afforded her a quick glance before addressing Rayad. She knew a few Arabic words, but the exchange was spoken so fast, none of it made much sense. Then Rayad seemingly barked out an order before pointing down the hall.

The man sent her an oddly apologetic look, lowered his head and continued on his way.

"What was that all about?" she asked after he disappeared.

"Your meal. I instructed him to place the tray in your room immediately after he asked if I had seen you. I told him you were standing before me."

Sunny shrugged. "That's understandable. He wouldn't have any reason to know me. I hope you weren't too hard on him."

"Only after he made the mistake of assuming you are my lover and not the sister of a princess."

She swallowed around her self-consciousness. "So he thought I was your mistress?"

"Precisely, yet he did apologize when I clarified your identity, although it was tempting to allow him to believe we are involved."

She leaned a shoulder against the wall as the need to be somewhat coy, even flirtatious, overcame her. "In your dreams."

He moved closer and nailed her with those damnable dark eyes. "I did have those dreams last night."

She playfully slapped at his arm like a fourteen-year-old with a first crush. "You did not."

He sent her a half smile. "Yes, I did. One cannot control the subconscious."

Clearly, she was having trouble controlling herself around him because at the moment, she really, really wanted to kiss him. "I agree with you on that. But I also know that you and I have no business dreaming about each other."

He inclined his head and studied her for a moment. "Did you have dreams of me?"

If only that were true. If only she were that well-adjusted. "Actually, no, but don't take offense. I was extremely tired and I fell asleep the moment my head hit the pillow." And that happened to be one colossal lie.

"My dreams of you were very interesting," he said, his voice low and compelling.

"In what way?"

He reached out and streamed a fingertip down her cheek, a gentle and almost comforting gesture, as if he sensed she needed that. "You were very spirited in my imaginings. I believe you are that way in all your endeavors."

Her recent past came crowding in on her. "At one time, I suppose I was, but lately that's not necessarily true."

"Is this due to lack of confidence due to your lover's disregard or has some other event changed you?"

His intuitiveness took her aback. Yet for the first time, she was very, very tempted to confess. "No, it's because…" She had no reason to tell him anything, though somehow she sensed he'd understand. "Let's just say things happen when you least expect it. Some not so great things, and we'll leave it at that."

After a brief bout of silence, Rayad took a step back. "Should you wish to speak to me of these *things*, it would be my honor to listen, and you may trust what you say will remain between us."

How badly she wanted to believe him, but she really couldn't. Not yet. "Thanks for the offer. I appreciate it."

He offered a warm smile. "I suppose you should return to your room before your meal turns cold."

"You're right," she said as she pushed away from the wall, clear disappointment in her tone. "Have a productive day."

"Will I see you tonight at the gathering?" he asked.

"Unfortunately, I'm required to make an appearance. But I only intend to stay long enough and mingle very little."

"If you are inclined, will you mingle with me?"

That would not be classified as a chore on any level. "I suppose I can add you to my dance card."

He frowned. "I do not believe there will be dancing at this event."

She laughed. "I know. That's just a saying…never mind."

He surprisingly clasped her hand and brought it to his lips for a soft kiss. "I will look forward to the moment when we meet again."

After he released her, Rayad turned and retreated in the opposite direction, leaving Sunny's mind in a serious state of confusion. She'd begun to discern a soft side to the tough guy, but perhaps his consideration only covered his true goal—seduction. She refused to fall in the frail-female trap. Or maybe she'd become too jaded to believe any man's motives. After all, she thought she'd known Cameron well, and she'd been terribly wrong. What true friend and former lover turned his back on someone in their hour of need? A man whose own guilt

overrode his compassion. A man looking for a way out
of a relationship that had grown static due to both parties' opposite goals and vast differences. She, in part,
had played a role in their demise by pushing him away.

If she ever decided to have a serious relationship
with someone else, Sunny vowed to choose a man who
believed in open, honest communication. She honestly
doubted Rayad Rostam would be that man because soul-
deep, she suspected he had his own serious flaws and
secrets.

Tonight she would converse with him, be cordial
and try her best to ignore his charms. How hard could
that be?

Four

The man's name should be Bond. Sheikh Bond.

Exactly Sunny's first thought when she glanced to her right to witness Rayad Rostam's grand entrance. She hadn't seen this much neck-craning since she'd been involved in a twenty-car pileup in Los Angeles.

He'd shaken and stirred almost every female in the packed ballroom—every size, shape, age and nationality—as they seemed to instantaneously notice the darkly gorgeous, debonair man dressed in black tie. She tried not to notice, honestly she did, but he was extremely hard to disregard.

When Sunny caught his glance, she refused to count herself among his admirers, even if she'd like nothing better than to go to him and request he take her away from the crowded ballroom. For that reason, she im-

mediately turned her attention back to Maysa Mehdi,
who looked beautiful in her flowing aqua gown, her
waist-length brown hair woven into a loose braid. She
also looked as if she could give birth at any minute. "Do
you need to sit down?"

The queen pressed a palm into her lower back. "I
need to go into labor."

"Hopefully not at this moment."

Maysa smiled. "That would definitely make the evening much more interesting."

Sunny couldn't argue that point. "When are you of-
ficially due?"

"Two weeks. As a physician, I know it's best if I
complete the gestation period. As a woman with swol-
len ankles, tomorrow would not be too soon."

Standing not far behind Maysa, Sunny noticed the
darkly handsome and somewhat fierce-looking man
she'd last seen at Piper and Adan's wedding reception.
"It seems Tarek Asmar is still on the guest list for all
important royal events."

"Yes, he is. My husband is quite impressed with his
business acumen."

"And that young woman seems quite impressed with
him, too."

Maysa subtly glanced over her shoulder. "That is
Kira. She basically runs the palace now that Elena has
decided to retire."

The woman looked as if she'd like to run off with the
billionaire. Or perhaps she was only being polite to an
honored guest. Nope. Sunny recognized serious flirta-
tion when she saw it.

Maysa presented a bona-fide frown, something she rarely did. "I believe you are being summoned, Sunny."

She followed the queen's gaze straight to Rayad, who was holding up the wall adjacent to the double doors, towering over several people in his vicinity. When he crooked a finger at her, she laid her hand above her breast and mouthed, "Me?" He answered with a nod.

She could fail to respond to the request, or she could see what he wanted. At the very least she should wait a bit so as not to appear too eager. But as if he'd morphed into some high-powered magnet, Rayad drew her toward him with only a sly, sexy smile.

As Sunny attempted to work her way through the crush of people, Piper clasped her arm, halting her forward progress. "Are you leaving so soon? We haven't even sat down for dinner yet."

Food wasn't quite as appealing as a striking guy in a tux. So much for ignoring Rayad. "I'm just going to grab some fresh air. It's a little warm in here."

"Will you be gone long?"

Not if she could help it. "I'll be back before the first course."

As soon as she reached Rayad, he clasped her hand and guided her to a corner away from the crowd. "May I say you look very beautiful tonight?"

She couldn't resist rolling her eyes. "Yes, you may, and I've heard that one before."

"It certainly bears repeating, and often."

Odd how he knew all the right things to say, and she felt the need to return the favor. "You look very handsome yourself, Your Highness."

He also looked as if he'd eaten a mouthful of pickled eel. "I prefer not to be burdened with an official title by someone with whom I have a personal connection."

They were definitely up close and personal at the moment, thanks to the middle-age woman wearing the purple silk caftan standing behind her, practically pushing Sunny into the sheikh. "All right, Rayad. Personally speaking, for such a thoroughly macho military guy, you wear refinement very well."

Amusement flashed in his dark eyes. "I truly appreciate your somewhat dubious compliment. Now if you would please come with me, I have something to show you."

All sorts of possibilities ran through Sunny's mind, none of which she could repeat in a social setting, unless it happened to be a biker bar. "Is it bigger than a breadbasket?"

Rayad's smile melted into a frown. "I am not quite clear on your meaning, yet I believe you will find it interesting."

Too bad she didn't know what *it* was, but her inherent sense of curiosity propelled her answer, and she couldn't discount the benefits of spending time with him. After all, she hadn't completely learned what made him tick. "I suppose I'm game since the noise in here is stifling. But you do realize if anyone sees us leaving together, rumors will spread like wildfire."

"They will only envy me due to my good fortune of having your company," he said, followed by the kind of grin that could drive a woman to write a poem in praise of his perfection.

But not her. Never her. She wasn't that taken with him. Much. "Since you put it that way, let's go."

As Sunny followed Rayad into the red-carpeted foyer, she cursed her apparent weakness where he was concerned. She ran through a mental laundry list outlining all the reasons why she couldn't become involved with him, if only temporarily. Reasons that hadn't existed until recently. Reasons she wished would just go away and allow her to be carefree again.

Together they navigated a labyrinth of hallways until they reached a steep, narrow staircase leading downward. "Is this the way to the dungeon?" she asked when Rayad stepped aside.

"No. It is a place of great historic interest."

That should make her feel better, but as she descended the stone steps on the stupid spiked heels, the claustrophobia began to hinder her breathing. Fortunately, the stairs weren't substantial in number, and she reached the bottom winded but without incident. Rayad joined her to open a heavy wood door, allowing her entry into a large room that resembled a museum, complete with glass cases.

"What is all this?" she asked him over one shoulder.

"Artifacts," he said as he walked to the display to her right. "The history of Bajul's past."

Sunny moved closer to him and studied the primitive pottery, glossy stones and weathered scrolls. "I'm no historian, but that all looks rather ancient."

"It is. Most of these relics were excavated in the desert region to the south of the mountains."

"That must have taken several years."

"It did take some time, yet it was worth my efforts."

She shot him a surprised look. "You found all this?"

"Yes. On the land I own approximately eighty kilometers from here."

While she mentally converted that into fifty miles, Sunny went back to surveying the artifacts. "Interesting. Is it a mountainous area?"

"No. The terrain is flat, and the climate much more arid."

One thing about Bajul—its topography was as varied as the state of Texas. "Do you prefer the desert?"

He inched a little closer to her side. "Yes. It holds a certain magic, particularly in the evening."

Cue the return of the midnight lovemaking fantasies. "Yes, it does. There's nothing quite like a warm breeze on your face while stargazing. I remember that from a trip to the Sahara."

"Would you wish to experience it again?"

"Experience what?" she asked, the rasp in her voice indicating her recent penchant for wicked yearnings.

"The desert and my land."

"Now?"

"Perhaps tomorrow would be better."

She called on her wit to cover the unsettling excitement. "Would we be traveling by camel?"

He released a low, sensual laugh that acted on Sunny like a potent aphrodisiac. "All-terrain vehicle. We could journey there during the day and return late into the evening."

She would be an absolute fool to agree. "Maybe that wouldn't be wise."

Taking her by the shoulders, he turned her to face him. "It would be very wise. The place I wish to take you is a healing sanctuary."

This time she laughed, a cynical one. "Honestly, my heart isn't that broken."

"Perhaps your soul is."

This conversation made little sense...unless... "Has Piper said something to you about my reasons for being here?"

"Yes, but you should not direct your anger at her."

Oh, but she would. "Piper had no right to tell you about the..." Even now she had trouble saying it. "What I went through."

He tenderly tucked a lock of her hair behind her ear. "If you feel it necessary to blame someone, then blame me. I sought her out to confirm what I suspected after our time in the garden."

She wasn't that transparent. Or was she? "I don't know how that's possible."

"I know the signs of trauma," he said. "You exhibited them several times, though you attempted to hide them from me."

She sighed. "Okay, I admit I've been jumpy since the incident. But I'll be fine. I just need a little more time."

He raised a brow. "Are you certain?"

Not exactly. "I've been told the memories will eventually pass."

"Allow me to assist you," he said as he cupped her jaw. "Allow me to take you to this safe haven. I expect nothing more than your company."

If only she could believe he had honorable intentions.

If only she wasn't waging her own war between accepting his friendship and wanting to feel whole again. To regain her inherent sensuality. Her trust. "I promise I'll think about it and give you an answer tomorrow."

He looked resolute. "You will go."

"You are entirely too confident."

"I know you better than you believe, Sunny. You once longed for adventure, yet your understandable fear prevents you from pursuing that which you desire. Let this journey be the catalyst to return you to who you once were."

Such a lofty goal. "You sincerely believe that will happen in one day?"

"With faith comes great reward, if you are open to all possibilities."

She was open to a lot of things, namely a kiss, yet she couldn't gauge how she might react. If the way he studied her mouth was any indication, she might find out. Instead, he took a slight step back and thrust his hands in his pockets.

"We should return to the reception," he said. "Otherwise, what I am considering could very well offend you."

"And that is?"

"I wish to kiss you, yet I do not wish to contribute to your discomfort due to my own cravings."

Hearing the words melted her resolve to stay strong and not succumb to his charms. Knowing he wanted her gave her unexpected courage. "I wouldn't exactly be uncomfortable, and I certainly wouldn't take offense. But I might regret it."

He smiled halfway. "Do you not trust my skill?"

She worried he had too much skill. "Oh, I trust you on that front. But how do I know you're not the kind of man who kisses and tells?"

His expression went suddenly somber. "Whatever transpires between us will remain between us."

Oh, heavens, she was going to do it—invite him to put her in a lip-lock. She had to know how it would feel. How she would feel. "In that case, show me your skill."

Keeping his arms to his sides, he leaned forward to press his lips against hers, making a brief pass, then another, as if testing the waters. Then, as if she'd become someone else, Sunny wrapped one hand around his neck, signaling she needed more. He answered that need by delving into her mouth with the soft glide of his tongue.

Skilled was an enormous understatement. The man was an expert. A kissing prodigy. She wanted to be closer to him, feel his arms around her. Yet when he drew her into an embrace, Rayad inadvertently triggered a series of frightening images from deep within her psyche—suffocating recollections that caused her to break the kiss and wrest away.

"I'm so sorry," she muttered around her labored breathing. When she noted the disappointment in his expression, she felt the need to explain. "This has nothing to do with you. It's me."

He narrowed his eyes and nailed her with a serious look. "What did your abductors do to you?"

"It's not what you're thinking." But it so easily could

have been, had she not had the good fortune to get away. "It's about the confinement."

He streaked a palm over the back of his neck. "My apologies for crossing a boundary I should not have crossed."

The sincerity in his tone touched her deeply, and led her to believe he truly was a "nice guy." "Rayad, I wanted you to kiss me, but I have serious issues due to the kidnapping. Maybe I'll tell you a few details to-morrow."

He couldn't mask his astonishment. "Then you will come with me?"

Rescinding her agreement seemed prudent. The urge to say "yes" won out over all her concerns. "All right. You win. I'll go."

He looked entirely too satisfied, and gorgeous. "We will leave before dawn so that we will have enough time to enjoy our day together."

Spending even a few hours in his presence seemed extremely appealing. "Then I suppose we should say good-night now so I can join my sister for dinner and get to bed a little earlier than planned."

"As much as I would like to stay with you a while longer, I will escort you back to the soiree for the eve-ning meal."

After they returned to the hallway in silence, Rayad gently clasped her hand, turned it over and kissed her wrist. "You will not regret your decision to spend the day with me."

She sincerely hoped not. "I guess I'll see you in the morning, bright and early."

"That will be my pleasure."

He turned and started away then paused and faced her again. "Bring a swimsuit with you."

That could pose a problem on several levels. "What if I didn't pack one?"

He brought out his best smile, and it was oh so good. "Then I suppose we will have to improvise."

With that, Rayad walked away, one hand in his pocket, the other dangling at his side, looking every bit the debonair devilish sheikh turned spy.

Sunny did own a swimsuit, and she'd brought it along. She also owned a scar she'd worked hard to hide. To most, it probably wouldn't appear that hideous, but it could lead to hard questions. And tomorrow she'd have to decide whether she would tell Rayad Rostam everything.

For the second time in two days, Sunny's dear sister had arrived at her suite to deliver a morning greeting, only this time she wasn't alone.

Piper stood in the corridor outside the guest suite with a sleepy baby, dressed in blue footed pajamas, resting on her shoulder. "I'm surprised you're up at this hour," she said as she breezed into the room. "I was walking this fussy little guy and thought I heard you stirring."

Sunny didn't care that Piper had stopped by or knocked loud enough to disrupt her sleep, had she been sleeping. She did have some measure of concern over what her twin would see. And after she saw it, the questions would start rolling in. Lots of questions. "Just thought I'd get an early start with my day."

When Piper laid little Sam on the unmade bed, the baby rolled to his belly with his knees bent beneath him, popped his thumb in his mouth and stuck his bottom in the air as if he wanted to show off the cartoon-airplane appliqué strategically positioned there.

So cute, Sunny's first thought. Such a big responsibility, her second. A responsibility she didn't welcome at this point in her life. Maybe someday she'd change her mind on her own without any pressure from those who believed it was past time for her to settle down.

As Piper turned from the bed, Sunny purposefully shook off the unwelcome recollections of her last argument with Cameron. But she couldn't shake the fact her sister was bound to see the evidence of her plans.

And no more had Sunny thought it, Piper did it— shot a look straight at the open bag set on the divan. She brought her attention back to Sunny, her blue eyes wide with surprise. "Are you going somewhere?"

She could lie, or she could play the avoidance game. "I'm not leaving permanently, if that's what you're asking."

"Are you going on an assignment?"

"In a manner of speaking, but it's not work-related."

"Are you being intentionally vague?"

Absolutely. "If you must know, I'm about to tour the countryside."

"Alone?"

Sunny brushed past Piper and shoved a couple of

T-shirts, a swimsuit and two pairs of shorts into the duffel. "No, mother hen. I have an escort."

"Do I know this escort?"

"Maybe."

"You're going with Rayad, aren't you?" Piper asked a little louder than necessary.

Sunny zipped up the bag, set it on the ground and turned to her meddlesome sister. "You might want to keep your voice down so you don't wake the baby."

"He can sleep through a sonic boom, and you haven't answered my question."

Time to reluctantly come clean. "Since I suppose you'll find out sooner or later, Rayad invited me to spend the day exploring his land."

Piper released a shrewd laugh. "I'm sure that's not all he wants to explore."

No matter how hard Sunny tried to fight it, a few wicked images invaded her brain. "Look, as bad as I hate to admit it, you were right. He's a nice guy. The perfect gentleman." And a stellar kisser. "Besides, you're the one who encouraged me to get to know him."

"True, but I thought if the two of you liked each other, maybe you'd start with dinner and a movie. I didn't expect you to go gallivanting all over Bajul with him for heaven knows how long."

"This is why I didn't want to tell you, Piper. You're blowing it way out of proportion. It's only a day trip."

"Then why are you packing extra clothes?"

Good question. "Because I like to be prepared, just in case."

"In case he wants to hold you captive?" Remorse

passed over Piper's expression the moment the sarcastic question left her mouth. "I'm so sorry. Poor choice of words."

Sunny hated pity of any kind, but she'd give her sister a free pass—at least on this count. "You don't have to evaluate everything you say to me, Piper. The abduction happened, and it's over. And while we're on that subject, why did you tell Rayad about it?"

"Because he came to me," she replied. "He sensed there was something going on with you beyond your breakup with Cameron. He also wants to help you with the aftereffects."

Now she wondered if Rayad's invitation had more to do with sympathy than with the desire for her company. A question she'd definitely ask him for the sake of clarity. "Like I said, he's a decent guy, and he expects me to meet him downstairs in less than twenty minutes. So if you don't mind, I need to dress."

Without saying another word, Piper gingerly picked up her sleeping son and returned him to her shoulder. "Just be careful, Sunny. I'd hate for you to have your heart shattered all over again."

Funny, her split with Cameron wounded her pride more than her heart. "Since I have no intention of getting involved with Rayad beyond a casual relationship, you have no need to be concerned."

Piper crossed the room, patting Sam's bottom as she went. "I didn't intend to fall for Adan, either." She paused at the door and smiled. "I want a full report when you get back this evening, and have fun. Just not too much fun."

With that, she disappeared, leaving Sunny alone to prepare for the trip with Rayad. She returned to the bag, opened it again and added a few travel-size toiletries, like they might somehow get stranded on a desert island, or perhaps in the desert. A ridiculous assumption, but he did mention swimming, so maybe it wasn't so far-fetched. She'd also learned the hard way that one never knew what the future might hold. And that unknown factor drew her in like a moth to a porch light. So did the prospect of spending the day getting to know Rayad even better.

The thought of an adventure exhilarated her. Thrilled her. If luck prevailed, she would have an experience she wouldn't soon forget, with a man she quite possibly would never forget.

Five

"Would you be so kind as to tell me where you are taking my sister-in-law?"

Leaning against the passenger door of the customized black Mercedes SUV, Rayad maintained his calm in light of Adan's heated tone. "Would you be so kind as to inform me why this is your concern?"

"She is my wife's sister, and she deserves to be treated with respect."

Rayad's own anger began to build, yet he refused to reveal it. "You may rest assured she will receive the utmost respect."

Adan pointed at him. "If you so much as make one inappropriate advance, you will have to deal with me."

As it had been when they were in their formidable years, he took great pleasure in tormenting his younger cousin. "Then I am to assume that I may make an *appropriate* advance?"

Adan's features turned fierce. "You bloody know what I mean, Rayad. No advances whatsoever. She is very fragile."

He would not describe Sunny as fragile. Wounded, yes. Fragile, never. "If it puts your mind at ease, Rafiq warned me to take care with her from the moment she arrived."

"My brother is a wise man," Adan said. "And if you find having both of us taking up verbal arms against you disconcerting, I promise you do not wish to deal with my wife."

That instilled more fear in Rayad than Bajul's entire armed forces setting their sights on him. "Again, you need not worry. We will only be gone for the day."

"I hope I didn't overpack."

Rayad turned his attention to Sunny standing behind Adan, a large olive-green bag clutched in her arms.

Adan shot him a suspicious glance and said, "I believe you stated you are going on a day trip."

"We are," Sunny said, a slight flush coloring her cheeks. "I'm one to prepare for any scenario, like a car breaking down. Earthquake. Monsoon. That sort of thing."

"You cannot be too prepared." Rayad opened the door and held out his hand to assist her. "Let us be on our way."

Adan glared at him. "I expect you to have her back here before dark."

After he helped Sunny into the Mercedes, he closed

the door and regarded his cousin again. "I have long since passed the time when I needed fatherly warnings, Adan. We will return when I see fit to return."

Without awaiting a response, Rayad rounded the vehicle, climbed into the driver's seat and turned the ignition. He sped away, glancing in the rearview mirror to find Adan still standing under the palace portico, appearing as if he would like to chase after them in his bathrobe.

"Nice ride," Sunny said as she ran a slender hand over the console dividing their seats.

The gesture, no matter how innocent, caused Rayad to shift slightly against the tightening in his groin. "It is adequate."

"I'd say the satellite radio, leather seats and moonroof qualify it as more than adequate. Company car?"

"Personal vehicle."

"I should be so lucky," she said. "My personal vehicle is a subcompact, but then I don't really drive that much."

He would gladly escort her anywhere she dared to go, particularly in a carnal sense. Yet he had to move slowly and accept that any intimacy between them might not come to pass.

Settling into silence, Rayad concentrated on navigating the steep descent away from the palace. Yet when Sunny's sigh drew his gaze, he saw her hide a yawn behind her hand. "You clearly are tired."

"Well, since the crack of dawn is still sealed," she began, "and I didn't get into bed until after midnight, I'm still a bit sleepy. But I'll wake up as soon as we get where we're going, wherever that is."

He felt the need to prepare her for the first step of their journey. "The place I am taking you will involve climbing, if you are willing."

"How much climbing?"

He sent her a glance to find her frowning. "Minimal, and I will assist you."

"As long as it's not Mount Everest, I can handle it."

He had no doubt she could.

When he noted the sky had begun to turn a lighter blue, he picked up speed, taking care to stay close to the side of the cliff as they ascended to their destination before they reached the village.

"Is it necessary to go this fast?" Sunny asked, a hint of concern in her tone.

"Only for a few more minutes."

And after those minutes passed, he pulled over at the road's bend and put the vehicle in Park. "We have arrived."

Rayad left the Mercedes and rounded the hood, only to find Sunny had exited without his aid. He knew better than to debate his duty as a gentleman. She was fiercely independent, one of the many aspects that had earned his admiration, though it warred with his protective nature.

As Sunny stretched her arms above her head, her shirt rode up above the waist of her beige cargo shorts, exposing bare skin that earned his immediate notice. "What now?"

He considered several answers to the query, yet what he desired to do, and what he should do, were in direct contrast with each other. "We will climb the precipice to your right."

She turned to survey the rock surface before presenting him with a less-than-pleased look. "It's definitely steep."

"Only from here. Once we begin our ascent, you will see it is not so difficult."

"If you say so," she said as she made a sweeping gesture toward the side of the mountain. "You go first, and I'll be right behind you."

Not at all what he had planned, yet he would refrain from arguing with her for the time being. "I will be happy to help you if the need arises."

"I appreciate your concern, but I have hiked quite a bit in my lifetime."

"Then perhaps it is time to test your skill."

She presented a smile that brightened her emerald eyes. "I'm always up for a challenge."

He happened to be up for several challenges, though one he did not particularly favor—resisting her feminine wiles. Yet he must resist so to prove he still retained some honor in light of his oftentimes dishonorable—though necessary—profession.

As the sky began to turn a pale blue, Rayad realized they would have to hurry to enjoy the advent of dawn. "Perhaps it would be best if you go first," he told her as he walked to the base of the rock wall. "I will remain close behind you."

She moved beside him and scowled. "To check out my butt, no doubt."

He had not considered anything but her safety, yet since she had mentioned it… "I wish to remain behind you in the event you stumble."

"And if I do, that means I'll fall back on you, and we could both plummet to our deaths."

"The peak is not as high as you might believe. If we fell, we might—"

"End up in a full body cast?"

"Suffer a few scrapes and bruises and possibly a broken bone."

"Or neck." She lifted her shoulders in a shrug. "But if you're willing to break my fall and be my cushion, who am I to argue?"

She smiled at him over one shoulder before she began to ascend the rock, carefully choosing her footholds, as if she had done this before. Perhaps she had, and that came as no true surprise to Rayad.

She fascinated him. She made him feel emotions he had long since learned to bury. She made him feel as if he were a whole man again. Many years had passed since he had experienced such strong, unwelcome emotions.

Surprisingly, she reached the top of the cliff with expediency, and once there, she turned and favored him with a smile. "You're as slow as a snail."

The insult sent him up to join her in a matter of seconds. "You clearly are a skilled climber," he said as he came face-to-face with her.

"I've done my share in some pretty rough regions, and apparently, so have you."

If she only knew where he had been, and what he had been forced to do at times, she would probably scurry back down the mountain and run to the palace. "I have, yet it is not often I have been graced with such a beautiful companion."

Her smile returned, soft and overtly sensuous. "And I've never known anyone who so easily threw out the compliments."

"Do not doubt my sincerity, Sunny, for as I have said before, I know true beauty."

With that in mind, he clasped her shoulders and turned her to face the east. The first fingers of light had begun to reveal themselves above the mountain range, giving the sky an orange cast. "This is why we are here. To pay homage to your namesake."

He remained close to her side to witness her reaction firsthand to that which he had so often taken for granted. Without speaking or moving, she stared at the sun as it rose in the distance. A warm breeze ruffled her blond hair, yet she seemed oblivious to her surroundings, and him. Though he should not be concerned by her inattention, for some reason he was.

"It's breathtaking," she finally said. "Seeing the dawn of a new day gives you hope that the world isn't such a terrible place after all."

Yet his world could be a terrible place on a constant basis. "I find this scene gives me a sense of peace, as well."

She sighed. "Sometimes peace is hard to come by so you look for it wherever you can find it."

He knew that to be all too true. "You will have peace again, Sunny. You are a survivor."

"Actually, you're right, and like I told you last night,

I'm going to be fine." The slight break in her voice belied her conviction.

"You are not yet *fine*, but you will be as soon as your
soul is on the mend."

She turned her gaze to his, a hint of frustration calling out from her green eyes. "Really, it's okay. As far
as I'm concerned, my breakup with the ex-boyfriend
was long overdue."

"I am referring to your abduction."

Rayad could tell by the way her body stiffened that
she relied on denial to dampen the memories. "I try not
to think about it too much for the sake of my sanity."

Sensing she needed comfort, he laid his palm against
her lower back, relieved when she did not recoil at his
touch. "There are certain experiences in life that haunt
us for many years. Circumstances that will lessen in
impact, yet never be entirely forgotten. Fortunately,
the passage of time does aid in gaining perspective."

"What events are haunting you, Rayad?"

Because his attempt at counsel had led to his trans-
parency, he would only supply a half-truth. "I am serving in the military. Oftentimes that regretfully entails
witnessing revolting acts imposed by men on other men.
Unfortunately, I am not at liberty to provide details."
Nor would he reveal his own personal tragedy.

"I understand." After a brief span of silence, she
asked, "Is that the baby-making mountain over there?"

That brought about his smile. "*Mabrúruk*. And yes,
if you believe in the legend, it has the power to render
women fertile within a hundred-mile radius."

"I'm not saying I believe in the legend, but would

you mind keeping your distance? Just in case." She followed the comment with a coy smile.

He did not care to keep his distance or acknowledge that he gave the folklore credence. "I do not believe that *Mabruk's* powers would enable me to impregnate you with only a touch of my hand."

"I suppose that would be miraculous."

"And it would take away the pleasure of the process of procreating."

Her cheeks flushed slightly as she lowered her eyes. "True. But the process doesn't have to be only about procreating, does it?"

"No, it does not." Should they continue this conversation, he might attempt to begin the process. Yet when it came to Sunny, vigilance should be paramount.

When she failed to speak, he felt an apology was in order. "I am sorry if I have upset you with my talk of procreation."

"Not at all," she said. "In fact, for the first time in a long time, I'm starting to feel like myself again. That kiss last night didn't hurt."

He tipped her chin up, forcing her to look at him. "If you believe nothing else about me, believe this. I would never intentionally do anything to make you uncomfortable."

"I know that, otherwise I wouldn't be with you. But there is something you can do for me."

"Whatever you wish."

"Kiss me good morning."

He struggled with what he wanted and what she needed. What he must do to win her trust so that he might guide her through the crisis. Yet refusing a beautiful woman's request for a kiss was foreign to him. Still, he vowed to proceed carefully from this point forward, and chose to press a chaste kiss against her lips.

She did not look at all pleased. "Very sweet. Not what I had in mind, but nice."

He cupped her cheek in his palm. "Had I kissed you the way I wish to kiss you, we might spend all day on this mountaintop. And though that might be pleasurable, we need to continue our adventure before the storms arrive."

Sunny turned her face to the skies. "I don't see even one cloud."

"The deluge is coming," he said. "But you will see no rain where I am taking you." A destination where he had never taken another woman since… He pushed away the bitter realities to focus on his companion.

"Can you give me just a little hint about where you're taking me aside from your land?"

"You will soon see for yourself. I will tell you it is unlike any place you have ever been before."

"I've been quite a few places."

"Trust me on this point."

"That remains to be seen."

Though she had said it with a touch of amusement, Rayad realized he would have to earn her confidence. And should anyone discover where he was taking her, he could be stripped of his duties and his honor, or worse.

Sunny McAdams would be worth the risk.

* * *

Rayad hadn't been kidding about the lack of rain. For the past twenty minutes, Sunny had yet to see any water whatsoever. The landscape had flattened into desert, the ground covered mostly in sand as far as the eye could see. Aside from one scant patch of grass supporting a small herd of sheep, the route they were taking showed few signs of population. And the farther they drove, the more desolate the surroundings became.

She adjusted in the seat to get a better look at Rayad and marveled at the perfection of his profile. The fit of his dark green T-shirt. She even sneaked a peek at his extremely masculine legs exposed because today he wore a pair of khaki cargo shorts and hiking boots. She also couldn't help but ponder the possibility of a real kiss later today—provided he actually cooperated. If she accomplished nothing else, she vowed to convince him she wasn't some broken, needy female who had to be treated with kid gloves. Okay, maybe she was a bit broken, but she felt as if she might be on the mend, thanks to him.

"So exactly where does your land begin?" she asked to disrupt the silence that had gone on way too long.

"We passed the property's boundary twenty miles ago."

"Wow." All she could think to say in light of the revelation. "You obviously own half of Bajul."

"Not quite half."

"How did you manage to wrangle the property away from the royal family?"

"A portion of the land was willed to me upon my

aunt's death. The rest I purchased since the area is not conducive for development."

"I can understand that. Most people don't care to live in the middle of nowhere."

"I am not most people."

That personal assessment wasn't remotely up for debate. "Is that why you haven't built your own palace?"

"I have no need for a palace," he said, his tone surprisingly serious. "I travel much of the time."

"I assume you have no need for a wife and kids, either."

"Not presently."

She would have sworn she heard a touch of wistfulness in his voice. "How much longer until we get where we're going?"

A split second after Sunny posed the query, Rayad took a sharp right turn and stopped the Mercedes in front of a fortress-like entrance, complete with barbed, ten-foot fencing. He then lifted the console, took out a remote control and pointed it at the heavy steel gate that opened wide to allow them entry.

She felt as if she were entering a prison and that resurrected memories she was hard-pressed to ignore. "What is this place? Some kind of military compound or maybe a sheikh commune?"

"You will see soon enough," he said as he drove forward.

If she wasn't so darned inquisitive, she might have demanded a better explanation before she allowed him to proceed. But crazy as it seemed, she didn't consider him threatening. "I'm looking forward to it."

They traveled down an afterthought dirt road that narrowed between two large stone formations. After threading the rocky needle, they finally reached a wider spot next to one of the behemoth boulders.

Rayad put the Mercedes in Park, turned off the ignition and shifted to face her. "Before we enter, you must promise me you will never speak of this place to anyone."

Sunny did a quick visual search but found nothing that even remotely resembled a structure. "I don't even see a *place*."

"Promise me."

Rayad's stern tone said he meant business. "All right," she conceded. "I promise to keep my mouth shut, like I do when I'm protecting an anonymous source. But if you want me to climb that wall, you should know I didn't bring any spikes or rappelling equipment."

"No climbing will be involved at this juncture." He opened the SUV door and told her, "Come with me."

When Rayad walked to the back of the Mercedes and retrieved what looked like a cooler, Sunny reached back to grab her own bag. She slid out of the seat and retraced his path, her mind caught in a web of confusion when he stopped in front of the mini-mountain. That confusion turned to blatant curiosity when he set the cooler down and opened a hidden panel set in the red-orange rock face, revealing a hi-tech keypad. While she looked on, he punched in a series of numbers, and just like that, the seemingly smooth stone parted. Definitely the stuff spy movies were made of. She wouldn't be a bit surprised to find a houseman greeting them with a tray of martinis.

After Rayad stepped aside, Sunny moved forward to find no servants, but she did discover another set of narrow stairs descending into darkness. Fortunately, this time she'd had enough sense to wear sneakers, not stilettos. Unfortunately, her heart began to beat at an accelerated clip when she noticed the narrow walls. "You seriously want me to go in there?"

"I promise it is safe."

She shifted the bag's strap to her shoulder. "No bats?"

"No. Or asps."

She could use some oxygen after hearing the reference to reptiles. "Thank goodness for small favors."

Rayad put the cooler down again, picked up a torch leaning against the wall, retrieved a lighter from his pocket and transferred the flame to a pair of sconces on either side of the steps. Then he turned and pressed a button to his left, closing the door behind him. "Follow me, and take care with your footing."

He certainly didn't have to worry about that. She'd take care all day long if necessary. While she followed behind him, Rayad lit more sconces as they traveled downward into the abyss. The scent of earth and a slight chill assaulted her. Luckily, she didn't smell fire and brimstone, although right now she wouldn't be surprised if they came across Hades.

Much to Sunny's relief, they eventually reached the final stair where she exhaled slowly when her feet hit the dirt floor.

Rayad paused and flipped a switch that illuminated several overhead lights, revealing a lengthy corridor. "A generator provides electricity, but I use it sparingly."

Sunny joined him and did a quick survey of the room to her right that held no real furnishings but a lot of electronics. "What is all this?"

"My means to communicate with the outside world."

Awareness began to dawn. "Is this a covert military installation?"

"In a manner of speaking," he said. "It's a natural bunker available for the royal family should Bajul come under attack. I discovered it several years ago."

"And that's when you found the artifacts."

"Yes. I have spent many days here exploring the surroundings and modifying the caverns to house occupants. I come here often when I am not on duty."

Now it all made sense. "So this is also your own personal hideout."

"Perhaps some would view it as such."

Including her. She couldn't help but wonder exactly what he might be hiding from. Granted, he'd claimed to be involved in military intelligence, but she sensed there might be more to the story. "Is this all there is to it?"

"No. I will show you the rest."

And he did, beginning with one room that held several bunks and what appeared to be an adjoining latrine. "This is huge. Do you sleep here?"

"I have my own private quarters that you will soon see, and you may leave your bag here."

She really didn't see much of anything other than a

long, narrow hallway. "Can't wait," she said as she set her duffel on the dirt floor by the door.

They continued on to a stockroom with rows of shelves holding what appeared to be military K-rations. A self-contained, primitive hostel. "I take it you don't have a refrigerator."

He placed the cooler on a table in the corner then faced her again. "No, but since the cave holds steady at fifty-eight degrees, spoilage is not an issue when I have fresh fruit delivered."

"All the way out here? That must cost a pretty penny."

"Money is not a concern when comfort is involved."

Of course it wasn't. The man probably had a fortune holed up in a wall somewhere. "Did you bring some fruit with you today?"

"Yes, and some other supplies," he said as he rejoined her in the corridor. "Should we require more, several outlying villages are not far away."

"Since we're only going to be here today, I'm sure we have enough to get us by."

"Perhaps," he said. "Let us now continue the tour."

After they traveled a few more feet, the hallway hit a dead end at another stone wall. Sunny assumed the tour was over, until once again Rayad revealed a keypad much like the one at the entry.

"What you have seen has been designed solely for security," he said. "What you will soon see is designed solely for pleasure."

He then punched in another code, and the walls parted like that proverbial Red Sea. The view he revealed absolutely stole her breath, but not because the area seemed confining. On the contrary, the place was massive—and mystical. The palace-size cavern, with glistening stones dotting the natural walls, could best be described as a fantastical, natural wonderland. Across the way, stalactites hung from the towering ceiling while stalagmites jutted up from the ground. And in the middle of the Caribbean-blue pool of water, a beam of light shone down from a large circular opening in the cave's roof.

A few moments passed before she recovered enough from her amazement to speak. "This is unbelievable. It reminds me of Jeita Grotto in Lebanon."

"Yet not quite as large," Rayad said from behind her. "And it is virtually untouched by man."

She couldn't seem to tear her gaze away from the remarkable sight. "It's truly a desert oasis. Where does the water originate?"

"From an aquifer fed by runoff from the mountains. Another of Bajul's hidden treasures."

Amazing. "Water is definitely in short supply in the region."

"That is why Zain has begun the conservation efforts. Eventually, it will be exported and in turn, secure the country's future, as well as save lives."

"Zain has seen what the lack of water can do to people. So have I."

She heard footsteps and sensed Rayad's presence before he said, "Are you not curious about my personal quarters?"

Sunny turned to find he was only a foot or so away. "Actually, I am."

"Then look behind me to my left."

Only then did she see the makeshift bedroom carved out of the rock. And on the raised ledge, a huge bed covered in dark blue satin and draped with a sheer canopy. A cave boudoir definitely fit for a prince. "Incredible. Do you have an en-suite bathroom? Maybe a steam shower and a whirlpool tub?"

He smiled. "Who needs those accoutrements when you have your own pool?"

"You bathe in the pool?"

"At times I have."

That unearthed some fairly naughty images involving a very masculine, well-toned body wet and slick with soap… "I suppose that makes you a modern caveman."

His low, sexy laugh echoed off the walls of the cavern. "I suppose that would be accurate."

She crossed her arms beneath her breasts against the onslaught of shivers, resulting from the cool temperature and his overt sensuality. "Well, as long as you don't beat me with a club and drag me by my hair, I can deal with that."

His expression went suddenly somber. "I would never do such a thing."

"It's a joke, Rayad."

"My apologies, but I find no humor in abusive behavior toward women."

Evidently he didn't bring his wit along with him. She also suspected a story existed behind his attitude. "I truly appreciate that. And in case I haven't said it before, I feel very safe with you."

Rayad surprised her by drawing her into a light embrace then rubbed his palm gently up and down her back. Funny, she hadn't even flinched, demonstrating how her trust in him had grown.

A few moments later, he framed her face in his palms and kissed her forehead. "Your faith means a great deal to me."

She smiled. "You're welcome. And now that you have me here, what's next?"

"We still have much to explore," he said as he kept his arms around her.

"Oh, really? What will we be exploring?"

"The cavern, of course."

"Too bad." Her face heated over her spontaneous comment. "I'm sorry. I meant I'm getting kind of hungry."

He stroked his knuckles softly up and down her cheek. "We will take a brief tour, then we will have lunch."

"Not that food in the supply room, I hope."

"No. I have brought something special from the palace." He studied her eyes. "I am very glad you are here."

"So am I."

And she was. By day's end, Sunny hoped that still remained true.

Six

He'd traveled through the tunnels many times before, yet seeing the cavern through Sunny's eyes made the experience seem new to Rayad. But when they had ended up in tight quarters several times, she had inadvertently brushed against him, stirring his body and his fantasies.

Even now, as he walked behind her and watched the gentle sway of her hips, he wanted her greatly. His fantasies took flight as he imagined Sunny naked, her long legs wrapped around his waist. He wanted to know how her bare flesh would feel against his palms, how she would feel surrounding him as he buried himself deep inside her.

Shaking off the images, Rayad remembered his vow to move slowly. He must accept that quite possibly nothing would come of his desire for her.

"Which way should I go?" she asked when they met a crossroads.

"To your right."

Once they emerged from the passageway, she turned to him and smiled. "We're back where we started."

"Yes, we are."

She snapped off the flashlight. "Any chance we can have lunch now? I'm really, really hungry."

As he was, but not only for food. "I suppose I could accommodate you."

"Gee, thanks. I'd hate to start foraging for wild berries since I doubt I'll find any."

"Berries actually are a possibility."

She rolled her eyes. "Please don't tell me we're about to trek through the desert to pick berries."

She brought about his smile that arrived more often in her presence. "No need for that. Now if you will follow me, I will bring our meal to you."

"Gladly."

He guided her around the bank of the aquifer and across the small wooden bridge he had built with his own hands. Once they reached his private quarters, he told her, "Wait here, and I shall return shortly."

"Hurry," she called out to him as he entered the bunker. "Or I'm going for the granola bars I brought with me."

He strode into the supply room to retrieve the container housing their meals. After he returned to Sunny, he nodded toward the pair of large crimson pillows next to the bed. "We will sit here to dine."

Sunny lowered herself onto the cushion and crossed

her legs before her. "I've heard of breakfast in bed, but never lunch next to the bed. So what's on the menu?"

After he took his place on the opposing pillow, Rayad opened the cooler, lifted the platter, set it between them and uncovered it. "This is the palace chef's specialty. *Shawarma* on taboon bread, topped with hummus and olives."

She picked up the sandwich, studied it briefly and then took a bite. "This is delicious," she said. "And I can't wait to dive into the dates and cheese."

He might have to dive into the nearby pool if he kept watching her mouth as she ate—and imagining how that lovely mouth would feel on his body. Instead, he handed her a bottled water, small silver plate and white cloth napkin. "Please eat as much as you would like. We have another tray for our dinner if this is not enough."

She paused midbite and frowned. "I thought we'd be heading back before dinner."

He tamped down his disappointment, with effort. "I had planned to have the evening meal here, beneath the stars."

Sunny mulled that over for a moment before she addressed him again. "I have to admit that sounds tempting, as long as you have me home before midnight in case I turn into a pumpkin."

"Pumpkin?"

She laid the sandwich down and dabbed at her mouth. "You know the story. Fairy godmother. Handsome prince. Young girl with evil stepsisters... Never mind. I tend to forget we're not culturally on the same page."

"Actually, I do know the fairy tale. Yet if my recollections are accurate, the young woman's gown turns to rags at midnight. I do not recall the threat of becoming a pumpkin."

Her laughter gave Rayad surprising joy. "Apparently, you can be very literal in your interpretation of folklore."

"Do you believe in these fairy tales?"

"If you're referring to happily-ever-after, I'm on the fence. My grandparents have been married for over fifty years and seem to still be in love. But my mother, and I use that term loosely, went from one man to the next, so obviously, she's never found what she was looking for in a relationship."

"And your father?"

She turned suddenly sullen. "I have no idea who he is. I did some investigating a few years back and after seeing the possible prospects, I gave up the search. Some things are better left unknown."

He would have to agree with that in terms of his past. "My parents have been wed over thirty years, although their marriage was arranged. However, they seem genuinely fond of each other."

"Fond isn't the same as love. I sincerely hope for Piper's sake that forever love does exist. But I'm certainly not looking for a charming prince to ride in to rescue me."

"You do not strike me as a woman who needs to be rescued."

"Are you sure that's not what this is all about?" she asked. "The noble sheikh attempting to save me?"

He would be foolish to believe he could save her when he had already failed another. Yet in some small way he needed to try in an effort to atone for his transgressions. "I am an ordinary man spending time with an extraordinary woman who needs a respite."

"You're definitely not ordinary, and I'm anything but special. But I do appreciate the compliment and that you're concerned about my well-being."

He reached out and touched her face. "As I have said before, I appreciate a beautiful woman whose humility prevents her from realizing her true worth. However, beauty is not only about physical traits. It involves the soul, even one that is injured. Yours might be wounded, yet it makes you no less attractive."

"Before we head in that direction," she began, "I'd rather talk about something more pleasant."

At some point he hoped she would talk to him about her experience. Since that would not happen in the imminent future, he opted for a suggestion that did not involve conversation. Perhaps not his first option but one that best suited her situation. "Would you wish to swim?"

She averted her eyes. "I'm not sure I'm ready for that."

"Did you not pack your suit as I suggested?"

"I have it." She finally raised her gaze to his. "I also have a reminder of my recent experience. A not so pretty scar."

"Show me."

"Maybe later."

Needing to encourage her, Rayad pulled his shirt

over his head and tossed it aside, revealing his own scars. "I received this six years ago," he said as he pointed to the jagged line on his left side. "The bruise on my right is from the broken ribs. On my back you will find a random pattern of slashes, compliments of a murderous insurgent who held me hostage and attempted to beat information from me."

Her green eyes widened. "How did you escape?"

Barely with his life. "My captor made the mistake of freeing my hands to move me to another chamber. He suffered a broken jaw for his efforts, and I managed to steal away without detection."

"I know all about fighting for freedom." Her tone hinted at a very real fear.

"Each scar we earn in our lifetimes has a story, Sunny. Every wound marks a challenge that we have overcome. If you will not show me your scar, then I implore you to tell me your story."

She drew in a deep breath and exhaled slowly. "If I do this, will you promise not to tell Piper the details?"

He worried the details were much worse than he had first presumed. "As I told you previously, what is shared between us, remains between us."

"I'll try to be brief."

"Take as much time as you need."

When a long span of silence passed, he thought she had reconsidered. Then finally she began to speak. "We were staying in a small village in Angola, covering a story on a group of aid workers. We knew going in that the area drew a dangerous criminal element due to the diamond trade. I don't think I realized how dangerous until that night."

As she hesitated again, Rayad took her hands into his. "You believe your attackers were a part of this element?"

She shook her head. "I'm not sure. I never saw them. They spoke broken English, and their accents had a Spanish note to them, but that's not what they were speaking because I know Spanish."

"How did you come upon them?"

She shifted on the pillow, a certain sign of discomfort. "Cameron and I were staying in a small bungalow in the center of the village. We'd had an argument about our future. He wanted to settle down and return to the U.S. and get married and have kids. I wasn't ready for that, and he knew it, but he kept pushing me. When I told him it might be best if we parted ways since we didn't want the same things, he demanded I leave and find somewhere else to spend the night. He insisted he didn't want to spend even one more minute in my presence. I decided to go for a walk until he calmed down."

He muttered an oath aimed at the man's disregard for his partner's safety. "He should not have allowed you to leave. He should have been the one to leave."

She sighed. "He realizes that now. He feels very guilty about the whole incident."

"As he should." In an effort to return to the abduction, Rayad asked, "What happened when you went on the walk?"

As if she could not tolerate the contact, she wrested her hand from his and gripped the pillow on either side of her thighs. "I was upset, so I wasn't aware of my surroundings. I passed by an alley and was ambushed. Someone pushed me to the ground and taped my mouth shut before I could even scream. They blindfolded me before I could get a good look, but I know there were at least two of them. One held me down, and the other tied me up."

"Is that where they kept you captive?" he asked, though he knew that most likely was not the case.

"No," she answered, confirming his suspicions. "Someone carried me to a small house, although I didn't know that at the time. I only knew I was put in some sort of tight space, like maybe a closet. I heard a door close, but I couldn't see a thing, and I could barely breathe, thanks to the tape on my mouth. I felt like I'd been buried alive."

"And that is the cause of your fear of enclosed spaces."

"Yes, it is," she continued. "I did get a periodic break when every now and then, I'd get yanked out, put in a chair and slapped around for unknown reasons other than I was an American journalist, or so I assumed."

His stomach pitched at the thought of anyone raising a hand to her. He had to pose a question that, depending on the answer, could change everything. A question he had presented Piper, yet he could not trust the answer. "Forgive me for asking, but were you sexually assaulted?"

She released a laugh that held no humor. "One of them tried. He came into that closet, closed the door and pawed me. He whispered things in my ear that I didn't understand, but I could just imagine what he was saying, and it wasn't pleasant. I still remember the way he smelled, like booze and sweat, as he climbed on top of me and tore at my clothes. I try not to think about it."

When Sunny seemed to mentally wander away, Rayad asked, "Do you wish to stop now?"

"There's more," she said, as if unburdening had become a total necessity. "The second time he came to me, he was more forceful, and that's when I started to realize it was only a matter of time before he…before it happened. And after that, I sensed they would kill me. The fight-or-flight response took over because I knew I had to find some way to escape."

"You fought him?"

She sent him a slight smile. "No. After he ripped the tape from my mouth, I knew what was going to occur if I didn't get away from him. I started to retch and told him I was going to throw up when he tried to kiss me, which wasn't far from the truth. I said I needed air or a bathroom or something. He dragged me out of the room by my wrists, pulled me to my feet then barked out an order to his partner. The next thing I knew I was being dragged somewhere. When I felt a breeze I realized I was outside, but I was terrified over what might transpire next."

"Clearly, you evaded them, or you would not be here," he said after a long pause in the conversation.

She drew in a ragged breath before continuing. "Luckily, my tormentor's partner untied my arms and legs, and that's when I saw my chance to kick and bolt. Before I could do that, I heard a voice whisper in my ear, 'Run.' And I did, as fast as I could. I stumbled while trying to remove the blindfold, but I recovered quickly and kept running. Then I heard the gunshot and a bullet whizzing by my head."

Rayad gritted his teeth against the force of his fury. "He gave you your freedom and then attempted to kill you?"

"It wasn't a *he*."

That temporarily shocked him into silence. "Your captor was a woman?"

"Yes, and I believe she wanted me to escape. I also believe she shot at me in an effort to convince her partner she tried to prevent me from getting away."

"After all that they did to you, you still believe in their humanity?"

"*Her* humanity. She may have been caught up in some Bonnie-and-Clyde scenario. She might have even been jealous that I was receiving her cohort's attention. I'll never know her motives or exactly why they targeted me."

"You believe these two were possibly lovers?"

"Maybe. I just remember him repeating the name Emma or maybe Erma, but it always sounded so sarcastic."

A possible clue to her abductors' nationality. "It was most likely *irmã*, Portuguese for *sister*."

"That would explain the accent and why she let him have his way with me. A sick sibling relationship for sure. Regardless, she did allow me the opportunity to escape, and for that I'm grateful."

Her attitude, though honorable, took him aback. "I

unfortunately cannot share your sense of compassion. I have no use for any person, male or female, who systematically tortures another."

She rested a palm on his forearm. "I can only imagine why you might feel that way in your line of work. But I have to continue to believe that most people are inherently good, or at least have some goodness in them. Otherwise, I might have totally withdrawn and stopped living for fear of running into bad guys around every corner. That is no way to exist."

He admired her strength. He appreciated her courage. He did have difficulty understanding her benevolence. "You're a brave woman, Sunny McAdams. Braver than many men I have known. Are you brave enough to show me your scar now?"

She came to her feet and gave him another smile. "Since you know the story behind it, I guess you should know it all. And since we're going swimming, you're going to see it all. So now I'll go change into my suit in the bunker, if you'll tell me how to open the disappearing door."

He stood and returned her smile. "Press the red button. It is unlocked."

"Okay." She turned then paused and faced him again. "I happen to love life, Rayad, and that makes me a survivor. I'm positive you're a survivor, too, and that's why we're drawn to each other."

When she walked away, he pondered her words. He had survived some of the worst scenarios, including one that had happened several years ago. Yet on that day, a part of his soul had died. He was not certain he would ever recover what was left of it, or to halt the search for the people who murdered his wife and child.

Sunny was surprised by how quickly she had revealed the details. Telling Rayad most of the abduction story surprisingly hadn't been that difficult, once she'd started talking. Wearing a swimsuit in front of him wasn't going to be quite as easy. He would then see remnants of the one detail she hadn't bothered to mention, though she wasn't quite sure why.

As soon as she'd put on the tasteful two-piece, her hand automatically went to the raised welt located right below her collarbone—and then came terrifying memories of the knife slicing her skin, followed by the warning issued by her terrorist in barely recognizable English.

Do as I say or next time, I cut higher.

She shook off the recollections as she wrapped herself in the towel she'd packed, holding it closed above the scar. Eventually, she would have to reveal it, but not until she was safely sequestered in water.

On that thought, Sunny made her way back to Rayad, careful to keep the towel clutched at her throat. But when she arrived, he was nowhere to be found.

Suddenly, he emerged from the reservoir like a gorgeous, golden-skinned god, a sensual smile curling the corners of his sexy mouth. He swam toward her until he found his footing and stood only a few inches from the stone bank. "I had begun to believe you had reconsidered."

She visually followed a droplet that trickled down

his sternum to where the water line circled his lower belly. She couldn't help but notice the beginnings of a thin stream of masculine hair traveling south from below his navel. She couldn't help but wonder if he was wearing swim trunks. "I haven't been gone that long."

"It seemed like an eternity."

Pretty words from a very pretty—in a macho sort of way—bad boy. "How's the water?"

"Temperate enough. Are you coming in, or do you wish to stand there and admire my aquatic skills?"

She'd been admiring a lot more than his skill a moment ago, and imagining all sorts of things. "If you're *that* good, maybe I should bow out and watch."

"If you do not swim all that well, I will assist you."

Sunny's competitive streak kicked, prompting a little temporary white lie in the form of playing the consummate helpless female. "How deep is it?"

"At the moment, I am standing on a narrow ledge that drops off into the depths behind me. I have never located the bottom, though I have tried."

She laid a dramatic hand above her breasts. "Wow. You're well over six feet, so that means it must be *really* deep."

"Do not be afraid."

She wasn't anything of the sort, and she planned to show him. With that in mind, she walked to the edge to study where Rayad was standing and to gauge the depth of the water behind him. Then in one fell swoop, she tore off the towel and executed a dive into the pool.

After Sunny surfaced several feet away from Rayad, she slicked her hair back with one hand and almost laughed when she saw the puzzled look on his face. Time to end the charade. "I happened to be on my high school swim team for four years, and I served as lifeguard during the summer. I've never been afraid of water."

Without saying a word, he shot toward her, using his long, powerful legs to consume the distance between them in a matter of seconds. "I suspected you were not being truthful," he said as he slid his arms around her.

She continued to tread water, well aware that not much separated them, both in space and in clothing, yet she wasn't the least bit afraid. In fact, her reaction had nothing to do with fear and everything to do with feminine need. At least he'd put on swim trunks so she wasn't tempted to act on those desires—yet. "I thought I'd done a pretty good acting job."

"Perhaps I know you well enough to see through your act."

That might not be up for debate since he'd demonstrated that on several occasions. "I'm sorry. I just couldn't resist raining on your macho-man parade. In case you haven't noticed, I'm rather self-sufficient."

His gaze traveled from her eyes to her chest, the scar plainly visible due to the clarity of the pool. "I have noticed your independence, and this." Keeping one arm around her, he slid his fingertips along the raised area. "He used a blade on you."

Rayad said it as a statement of fact, not a question, but he still looked as if he needed her confirmation. She saw no real reason not to explain at this point. "Yes, he did. Or that's what I assume since I couldn't see it. But

I definitely felt it. If I hadn't cooperated, he promised to be more accurate the next time."

"The scar is not as unsightly as you might think."

"It's bad enough, but I'm getting used to it. Besides, it gives me a good excuse to buy a new necklace."

His smile indicated he might actually appreciate her sarcasm. "Perhaps I will purchase that for you, although you should wear your wound proudly as a sign you had the strength to survive."

Exactly what she'd planned to do—eventually. Unfortunately, she didn't feel all that strong at the moment. Not with Rayad so close, her hands resting on his broad shoulders while her heart beat a staccato rhythm in her chest. "Are we going to just float around here like a couple of rafts, or are we going to swim?"

He pressed a soft kiss on her cheek. "How is your endurance?"

"I don't know. How's yours?"

"Excellent. I am also able to swim long distances, as well."

The sexy devil. "What do you have in mind? From a swimming standpoint."

He looked thoroughly disappointed. "I have somewhere else to show you, but we can only see it by water."

"Sounds interesting. You lead, I'll follow."

This time he landed his lips square on her mouth, but he didn't linger very long. "When we reach the opening to the cavern, take hold of my leg."

"Is that really necessary?"

"Do you wish to be lost?"

He had her on that one. "No."

"Should you inadvertently let go, you will be in total darkness. Keep going as you will shortly return to light, and our destination. I will go slowly."

She brushed a kiss across his unshaven chin. "Don't be careful on my account."

He responded with an all-out grin. "Are you ready?"

"I'm ready."

Before she could draw another breath, Rayad took off, swimming toward the mouth of the cave they had explored earlier. She attempted to match him, stroke for stroke, but he was just too fast.

By the time she came upon the abyss, he was waiting for her, looking as fit as a fiddle and ready to take on the English Channel. She, however, was a bit out of shape. "That was exhilarating. How much farther?"

"Not very far at all."

"Apparently your ribs have sufficiently healed."

"Well enough. Now take hold of me and do not let go."

Ever the tough guy. She gave him a salute. "Aye, aye, captain."

Rather than hinder his movements by commandeering his leg, Sunny slid her hand in the back waistband of his trunks. She only caught a glimpse of the scars, but they couldn't detract from his appeal regardless of how bad they might be. Nothing could ever take away from the fact he was a compassionate, strong and extremely desirable man.

As Rayad guided them through the darkness, Sunny had a few moments of knee-jerk distress. But it didn't take long before she allowed herself to enjoy the free-

dom, the sounds and scents of the cavern and the man
serving as her own personal escort through paradise.
She soon became aware of the fact she didn't feel the
least bit claustrophobic, despite the total blindness to
her surroundings. Instead, she felt oddly elated, completely liberated and oh, so taken with Rayad's con-
trolled strokes, bringing to mind some other strokes
she would like to experience.

Down, Sunny—her thought as they continued on
their trek. She needed to be a bit more wary, otherwise
she would end up going down the wrong road with
Rayad. Or maybe it could turn out to be the right road.
Only time would tell.

The blackness began to fade as they rounded a bend,
and a large opening revealed a gentle waterfall flowing
down the stone, feeding the basin below that led to the
underground aquifer.

Sunny let go of Rayad to swim forward, and when
she felt sand beneath her feet, stood to admire the scene.
"This is absolutely breathtaking."

"Yes, it is."

She looked back to find him staring at her. "I'm sure
you've seen it so many times, you take it for granted."

He waded toward her and paused at her side. "I still
appreciate its majesty, but I was not referring to the
falls."

"Did you mean the sun bouncing off the water? The
blue, blue skies?"

"My admiration is solely for you."

She faced him and faked a frown. "You are one
charming sheikh."

"And you are one very stunning woman."

"Flattery could very well get you anywhere you want to go," she said as she draped her arms around his neck.

"Anywhere?"

Time to rephrase that. "Okay, anywhere we both mutually decide to go."

"Do you have a place in mind?"

She felt a little bit giddy and a whole lot bold. "Why don't you kiss me, and we'll find out?"

He did. A coaxing kiss, but very persuasive. He sent his palms down her sides slowly then back up again and paused precariously close to her breasts. She could tell him to stop, or she could encourage him to go. She wanted him to go, not stop.

More brazen than she'd ever been before, Sunny reached back and unfastened the clasp at her back, then loosened the tie at her neck, allowing the swimsuit top to drop and float away.

Apparently aware that she was now bare from the waist up, Rayad broke the kiss and favored her with a knowing smile. He cupped her breasts, circling his thumbs around her nipples while seemingly studying all the details. She wasn't overly endowed like her twin, but the gentle way he treated her, she couldn't care less.

Never had she let a man she'd known for such a short time go this far this fast. Did that make her more like her mother than she cared to admit? She didn't want to think about that now. She stopped thinking altogether when Rayad lowered his head and replaced one hand with his lips.

The sensations were remarkable, from the pull of

his mouth to the flick of his tongue. Waves of heat washed over her and settled between her thighs. As if Rayad sensed that, he pulled her legs up around his waist, bringing her in close contact with his very impressive erection. Then he began to move her up and down against his groin, creating a friction that brought her close to the edge of climax. If he kept it up, she would start making a few primitive sounds, or beg him to put her out of her misery. Then he had the audacity to stop moving altogether.

After Rayad set her back on her feet, Sunny bit her tongue to keep from cursing. "Nothing quite like getting turned on then immediately turned off."

He swept a hand over the back of his neck. "That was not my intention. If I had my way, I would have taken you here without formality."

That sounded like a good plan to her. "Why didn't you?"

"I am not certain this is what you want."

She crossed her arms over her bare breasts and blew out an impatient sigh. "Believe me, I'm not that good at faking it."

He retrieved her top that was floating nearby and handed it to her. "When a person has a brush with death or suffers a loss, at times they search for any means to remind themselves they are still alive."

She redressed and refastened her suit, all the while battling frustration. "Is that truly what you think I'm doing?"

"I believe it is possible."

She viewed his concerns as an affront to her character. "For your information, I'm not the kind of woman who goes searching for just anyone to meet my needs, physical or emotional. If I didn't trust you, I would never even consider crossing the intimacy line. Believe it or not, I do trust you, Rayad, and I want you more than I've wanted any man in a long time, even Cameron. If that's crazy, then I'm certifiable. But I can't help how I feel."

Some unnamed emotion reflected from his eyes. "I truly appreciate your continued faith in me, yet trust should be earned."

"You earned it when you halted our little interlude because you're worried about me. However, something tells me there's more to your worries than whether or not I'm ready. Maybe you're the one who isn't ready."

He took her hands in his and gave her a meaningful look. "It has been some time since I have been with a woman, yet my concerns lie solely with your well-being. If you decide we should enjoy each other from a carnal standpoint, you may rest assured I will grant you an experience that you will not soon forget. Although I am not averse to lovemaking in various places, our first time should be in a proper bed."

She found his self-assurance and traditional ideals oddly appealing, and believable. "Then we're agreed that when the time comes, we let nature take its course with no more second-guessing?"

His expression brightened a bit. "Agreed. You only have to ask, and I will answer your every fantasy."

Even with the sun beating down on her head, she experienced a bout of chills when she imagined him stealing into her suite tonight once they returned to the palace. And on that note… "I suppose we should think about heading back before dark. I'd like to be there in time to have dinner with Piper."

"We will dine here before we return."

Spending a few more hours in his presence in this secluded place wasn't such an awful prospect. Not in the least. Maybe she wouldn't even have to wait to fulfill her fantasies. "We can stay." She pointed at him. "And you better really have a tray from the palace, not serving me something from one of those cans on the shelf."

His grin arrived full-throttle. "You will find the fare more than adequate."

She found him utterly irresistible. "Out of curiosity, exactly where are we having dinner? Next to your bed?"

"No." He lifted her hands and brushed a soft kiss on each of them, like some chivalrous Arabian knight. "Per my original plan, we shall dine beneath the stars."

Normally, she didn't require romantic gestures, but with Rayad, she wasn't quite herself. "That sounds wonderful."

"Rest assured, it will be," he said. "And afterward, I will safely escort you back to the palace."

As far as Sunny was concerned, she didn't care if they were detained for the evening, as long as he made good on his promise to fulfill all her fantasies. In doing so, she could experience one very *hot* desert night.

Seven

They would not be returning to the palace tonight.

Rayad dreaded telling Sunny the news for fear she would not believe him. Prolonging the inevitable would not change the situation, and that truth sent him from the radio station to seek her out in the sleeping quarters where she had retired two hours ago.

When he entered, he found her on a bunk curled up on her side, her eyes closed against the dim overhead light. She looked so peaceful, he hated to wake her. Instead, he perched on the edge of the narrow bed next to hers to watch her a few moments, while she was unaware.

He had never known anyone quite like the courageous journalist. He had rarely been so quickly affected by a woman. His craving for her was both foreign and undeniable. Even now, the temptation to strip out of his clothes and join her lived strong within him. He refused to do that for many reasons. Although she had insisted she would gladly welcome him into her bed, he still had reservations. Should she ever discover the capacity in which he served his country, she would never view him the same way again. She would undoubtedly never trust him again.

Perhaps he should reconsider their evening together. Perhaps he should have returned her to the palace immediately before it had been to late to do so.

Yet when Sunny began to stir and after her eyes fluttered open, all thoughts of what should have been disappeared And when she greeted him with a soft smile., he could only consider how badly he desired her. "How long have you been sitting there?" she asked, her voice hoarse from sleep.

"Not long."

She stretched her arms above her head and sighed. "What time is it?"

"Sixteen hundred hours."

Her smile disappeared. "I'm still not fully awake. Regular time, please."

"4 p.m."

"Really?" She sat up against the metal headboard. "I didn't mean to nap that long. You should've woken me."

He had wanted to do that very thing in some very creative ways. "You were tired from the day's activities."

"True. So what's on the agenda between now and dinnertime?"

"I will be traveling to the closest village to the south

to purchase supplies. Feel free to continue your nap in my absence."

"What about the dinner you brought with you?"

The time had come to reveal the weather issue. "I received some recent news from Rafiq that prompted my decision to travel to the village."

"Are you buying souvenirs?"

"No."

Her green eyes widened. "Is the baby coming?"

"He did not mention the child or his wife, so I assume not."

She blew out a frustrated breath. "I'm not in the mood to play a guessing game, so just tell me what he said and why you have to go shopping when it's obvious you have tonight's meal."

He leaned forward, rested his arms on his legs and laced his fingers together between his parted knees. "It appears the storms are worse than first predicted. The flooding has been extensive, and it has required ground troops to evacuate the villagers to higher ground."

"Is anyone in the palace in danger?" she said, her tone hinting at alarm.

"The palace is elevated enough not to suffer any ill effects. However, the roads into the village are currently impassable."

"That means we're stuck?"

He did not care for the word *stuck*. "We will be confined here until the passage is clear."

She fell back onto the pillow and studied the stone ceiling. "How long before we can go back?"

"Three days minimum. Possibly longer."

"Great."

Her annoyance did not please him. "Do you find spending an extended period of time with me completely unpalatable?"

She sent him a sideways glance. "I didn't say that. I just feel bad that I haven't spent much time with my sister. Not to mention I only have two days' worth of clothes. Unless you have a laundry hidden somewhere, that could pose a problem since washing my stuff in the aquifer isn't exactly eco-friendly."

Her reasoning gave him some measure of relief. "I will purchase what you need in the village."

She seemed insulted by his offer. "I have my own funds, Rayad. Of course, if they don't take credit cards—"

"They do not. Therefore, you will need to allow me to assist you. Or perhaps you would like to borrow clothing from me."

"If your clothes fit me, then I seriously need to consider a diet."

She was perfect in every way that counted, in his opinion. "My shirts might be large, but they would adequately cover you."

"Yes, but there is the underwear issue."

He almost proposed she not wear any. "Again, you will find all you need in the village. I will escort you there first thing in the morning."

"Fine, but that doesn't ease my guilt over abandoning Piper when she was so kind to invite me."

Knowing Sunny would be leaving soon gave him cause for concern, though he could not say why. He had known all along that her departure was inevitable, as was his return to his duties. Still, their parting bothered him on a level he would have to examine later. "You will have ample time to visit your sister, unless you plan to immediately return to the States once we arrive back at the palace."

"I'll be staying for another couple of weeks." She pushed off the bed, rifled through the bag set on the floor and withdrew a brush. "If you're going shopping, then I might as well go with you now to pick up what I need. Besides, I don't want to stay here alone because I'm still not convinced I won't come across a bat or two."

He would like nothing better than to have her company. "Then you are not angry with me over the delay?"

She stroked the brush through her silken blond hair several times before contacting his gaze. "You have no control over the weather, Rayad. You might be a powerful guy, but you're not that powerful."

He had a powerful urge to kiss her—after he divested her of the white shirt and brown shorts. "I promise you will not have to concern yourself with my behavior during the remainder of our time together. You are still in complete control."

She paused the brush midstroke and smiled again. "I'm not sure I can promise you the same thing when it comes to my behavior. You have a way of making me lose control."

If he did not retreat soon, he would not be able to disguise his burgeoning erection, compromising his dignity. "We should travel to the village now while it is still daylight," he said as he stood.

Sunny tossed the brush back into the bag, slid her arms around his waist and pressed a kiss on his lips. "I'm ready to go shopping. And I'm really ready for our dinner beneath the stars."

So was Rayad. He only hoped he could keep his baser urges in check long enough to finish their meal. After that, he would make no promises.

The small village marketplace had been surprisingly crowded with men dressed in traditional *thawb* and women wearing *abayas*. Sunny had only seen a handful of vehicles, but a lot of livestock—from cows to camels. The smells of spices and grilling meats coming from small tents set up by vendors had made her incredibly hungry. Her darkly handsome escort had also fueled her appetites that had nothing to do with dinner.

Several times during the trip, Sunny had almost lost Rayad in the crowd. The language barrier had hindered her ability to understand his conversations with the locals, and he'd had plenty. Yet one thing she had understood— they'd called him Basil. Later this evening she would answer her curiosity and ask him why they didn't use his proper name. Why they seemed to treat him like a fellow commoner, not well-heeled royalty.

Right then, she had to haul all the supplies out of the Mercedes while Rayad opened the secret door. Cave, sweet cave. The thought made her smile.

"What do you find so humorous?" he asked when he joined her at the rear of the vehicle.

"Nothing," she said. "Just glad to be back and glad I have my own personal pack mule."

He faked a frown when she handed him two of the burlap totes. "Are you calling me an ass?"

"Not at all. But I do like your ass." She topped off the comment by patting his cargo-pant-covered bottom and heading toward the entry.

By the time they made two trips up and down the stairs, Sunny wanted nothing more than to take a bath. "Am I supposed to clean up in the reservoir?" she asked as she laid the caftans Rayad had bought her on one bunk.

"You may, or you may use one of the showers."

Clearly he'd been withholding pertinent information. "You said you didn't have a shower."

"Not adjacent to my quarters." He pointed across the room at a closed door. "You will find one in there. The pressure is adequate although the water will be cold."

She swept one arm across the perspiration beading on her forehead. "A cold shower sounds perfect. I'm still trying to recover from the heat." He wouldn't help her body temperature one bit if he kept standing there with his arms folded across his chest, the short sleeves of his black tee revealing biceps that should be registered as lethal weapons. Yep, a cold shower was definitely in order.

"I will leave you to your bathing now while I prepare our meal."

She hadn't realized how hungry she was until he'd mentioned that. "Great. I shouldn't be long since I didn't pack the hair dryer."

He smiled before he started away then paused and faced her again. "Perhaps at some point in time during our stay together, I will join you in the shower."

With that, he left the bunk room, closing the door behind him, and leaving Sunny with all sorts of questionable ideas and mental images. She couldn't wait to be alone with him under the night skies. She couldn't wait to see what might transpire after dinner. Then again, she could be disappointed if he brought out the honor card.

Fortunately, she had ways to convince him to take the next step, beginning with making herself fresh and presentable. She made quick work of the shower that was more of a stream, thankful she brought shampoo and bath gel. She then grabbed a towel from the metal locker, dried off and returned to the room to retrieve her favorite sleeveless gauze caftan.

As she held it up, she did a double take when she noticed the wide silver necklace intertwined with deep coral beads that perfectly matched the color of the dress. She had admired it, but she certainly hadn't purchased it due to her lack of cash, not to mention the rarity of the stones that carried a hefty price tag. Instead, she allowed Rayad to buy her a pair of sterling hoops that were much less expensive after he insisted.

No doubt he'd been the jewelry culprit, and she would definitely thank him, argue it was too extravagant, and then maybe show her appreciation with a big, fat kiss.

After she twisted her damp hair into a loose braid, Sunny slipped into a pair of the recently purchased sheer white muslin underwear that looked like men's boxers, only shorter. Not exactly sexy, but functional. Luckily, the dress didn't require a bra. She then applied a little mascara and lip gloss using a compact mirror, slid the earrings into her lobes, clasped the necklace around her neck and marveled over the fact she had morphed into a girly-girl. Piper would be so proud. Piper would also hate that her twin didn't have a pair of spiky heels at her disposal. Thank heavens. Barefoot seemed to be the way to go in lieu of sneakers, although she worried she might wind up with a stubbed toe, or step on a snake.

Satisfied everything was in place, Sunny walked into the corridor to find Rayad standing by the entry to the cavern. He'd changed into a plain white tee and dark blue cargo pants, and it appeared he had shaved his beard down to a shadow. One gorgeous, gorgeous man at her disposal. Lucky her.

She executed a corny curtsey. "Good evening, Your Highness. You clean up good."

He nodded slightly. "As do you. The dress fits you to perfection, yet I knew it would."

She figured he'd had a lot of experience with gauging a woman's size. He'd probably had a lot of experience with a lot of women. "Thank you," she said, her face flushed. "Since it's getting fairly late, is dinner ready?"

"It is," he said. "Now if you will follow me, I will show you to our private dining room."

Sunny wasn't too thrilled to have to climb yet another flight of stairs. But the effort was well worth it when they emerged at the top of the rock formation and stepped onto a sandy plateau. Her attention immediately turned to the host of diamond-like stars spread out as far as the eye could see, and the near-full moon hanging high overhead. An amazing panorama and the perfect start to an equally amazing night. "I'd forgotten how incredible the night sky looks in such a remote place."

Rayad slid his arms around her from behind. "I am sorry we missed the sunset, but perhaps we will see that before we return to the palace."

She didn't even want to consider leaving this place, or him. Leaning back against his chest, she caught a whiff of what must be his soap, a heady scent that reminded her of exotic incense. Not only did he look great and feel great, he smelled great. "Who needs the sun when you have all these stars?"

"We both need sustenance."

She turned into his arms and smiled. "That would probably be a good idea. Otherwise, you might have to carry me back down those steps."

He feathered a kiss on her forehead. "That would be my pleasure. Yet I would not want to stop until we reached my bed."

"Maybe I wouldn't want you to stop."

"That is good to know, as long as you are certain that is what you wish."

She couldn't quite peg why he continued to need reassurance, unless it had more to do with his reticence. Regardless, she would provide it. "Believe me, that's exactly what I wish."

He kissed her then—a long, lingering kiss that made her forget all about dinner. She focused on the feel of his tongue softly exploring her mouth and his palms roving up and down her back before coming to rest on her bottom. She remembered their sexy interval in the pool and realized if they didn't quit now, they might ignite the sand beneath their feet.

As much as she hated to do it, Sunny broke the kiss and said, "Maybe we should grab a bite to eat."

He released her and cleared his throat. "That would probably be advisable."

"Probably so."

Taking her by the hand, he led her to an area illuminated by a lone torch set into the ground. A multicolored blanket held various platters with cheeses and meats and fruit, along with a basket of bread.

Sunny's returning appetite caused her to let him go and drop down onto one of the pillows flanking the food.

After Rayad joined her on the opposing cushion, he handed her a plate. "As they would say in America, dig in."

She laughed. "Yes, that's what they would say. And yes, I gladly will."

Every bite Sunny took was pure bliss, though she couldn't say if she was driven by hunger or simply the atmosphere. They barely said two words during the meal, and before long, they'd made quite a dent in the food.

She wiped her mouth with a napkin and moved her empty plate to the middle of the blanket. "That was the best meal I've had in years."

Rayad pushed the pillow away and stretched out on his side, using his palm to support his jaw. "Do not become too accustomed to this luxury. What I have brought from the market is simple."

She briefly studied the night sky and relished the warm breeze blowing across her face. "I don't care what we eat as long as we eat it here." When she brought her attention back to him, she found him staring at her intently. "What? Do I have something on my mouth?"

"You have a beautiful mouth," he said. "And I see nothing obstructing my view of it."

She set her pillow aside and stretched out to face him, leaving little space between them. "Considering how busy our day has been, you'd think I'd be tired, even after my nap. But remarkably I'm not. And that reminds me, I have something to ask you about our trip to the village."

"I will answer to the best of my ability."

Time to play the name game. "When we were in the village, I thought I heard people calling you Basil. Did I misunderstand?"

"No, you did not. That is how they know me."

"Then they don't realize you're a prince?"

"They do not, and that is how I wish it to be."

"Why?"

"One never knows where enemies might be lurking. It is best to blend in with the masses and conceal your true identity."

Now it made sense. "Ah, it's that whole 'spy guy' thing. And by the way, you never have told me your code name."

"If I did, I would have to—"

"Kill me?"

A strange, almost wary look passed over his expression before he quickly replaced it with a smile. "I would prefer to kiss you." And he did, soft and slow and much too short, before he asked, "What do you wish to do now?"

A very loaded question. "What do you wish to do?"

"I cannot tell you what I wish to do for fear you might leave."

She scooted closer. "Try me."

"I would rather show you. Lie back."

After Sunny complied, Rayad rose above her and studied her face for a long moment. The next kiss he delivered was tempered at first, then deeper, and grew predictably hotter.

He broke away long enough to remove his shirt, then quickly divested her of the caftan. When he took her back into his arms and kissed her again, the feel of his bare chest pressed against her breasts caused her to shift restlessly against the dampness between her thighs. She wanted nothing more than to have him relieve the ache, but he'd told her she would have to ask. She could do that. Better still, she could follow his lead and point him in the right direction.

On that thought, Sunny lifted Rayad's hand from the curve of her hip, placed it on her inner thigh then held her breath while she waited for him to respond. She didn't have to wait long until he skimmed his palm higher up her leg, pausing to toy with the bottom edge of the unflattering underwear, as if determined to tease her into oblivion. A needy sound slipped out without

regard for her effort to stop it, and that involuntary reaction seemed to send Rayad into action.

In one smooth move, he had her muslin pants pushed
down to her knees and his hand between her legs. He
continued to kiss her, his tongue mimicking the move-
ment of the stroke of his finger, stoking a fire that
threatened to sear all her control.

He took his mouth away and whispered, "You are
very wet," without missing a beat with his touch.

If she could find her voice, she'd probably respond
with "You think?" but she was too far gone to speak.
She couldn't do anything but give in to the sensations
and brace for the impending orgasm. It came swift and
hard in a series of strong spasms that caused her to
tremble all over.

Sunny gradually returned to reality when Rayad
rained kisses on her face, but her respiration still wasn't
quite steady. "Wow," she managed to say after a time.

"Did you find that satisfactory?" he asked.

"Do politicians play favorites?"

His laugh rumbled low in his chest. "That was only
a sample of what I will do for you. There will be more
to come, if you so desire."

You betcha she did. "I'm not sure I can handle much
more."

He ran a fingertip along her jawline. "You can handle
more than you realize. You will eventually see that."

At the moment, all she could see was stars, and not
just the ones glimmering above her. "I'm going to take
your word for that." Feeling unexpectedly bold, she
rolled to her side to face him. "Take down your pants."

The demand evidently shocked him momentarily into silence. "Do you wish me to leave on my boots?"

She rose up and nudged him onto his back. "I said take down your pants, not take them off. Then you don't have to worry about your shoes."

"But—"

"No buts," she said as she wagged a finger at him. "As women say in America, do as you're told, sit back and enjoy it."

That unearthed his sexy smile. "Far be it for me to question a determined American woman."

While Rayad undid his fly, Sunny kicked out of the underpants before turning back to him to see he'd pushed his pants to his knees.

Amazing. The man had been endowed with many physical gifts, and she just discovered another one. He was mighty proud to see her. Very proud. He had every right to be.

After laying her cheek on his chest, she drew a line from his sternum down to his abdomen then lightly raked her nails up his thighs. He remained very still and silent, until she set out to explore him from shaft to tip. His indrawn breath indicated she must be doing something right, so she kept right on doing it. And when she circled her hand around him, he released a groan. That chink in his armor drove her to continue to stroke him, knowing that it wouldn't take much to send him completely over the edge. But before she could, he clasped her wrists and wrested her hand away.

"Enough," he said, his voice bordering on a growl.

She raised her head to find his eyes were closed. "Did I do something wrong?"

"On the contrary, you did everything right. That is why I stopped you."

"I think it's only fair that I return the favor."

"I prefer you not."

She felt suddenly self-conscious, and a tad miffed. "Does it bother you when a woman takes control and causes you to lose control?"

"That is not my concern."

Here we go again. "Look, if you're going to start spewing that stuff about me not knowing my own mind—"

"I was going to say that I want to be inside you."

Well, that changed everything. "I'd like that a lot."

"As long as I know you are certain you wish to proceed."

The last of her patience floated away on the warm desert breeze. "I am completely naked and still riding the pleasure train after having one of the best orgasms of my life. That pretty much speaks to my certainty."

Finally, he looked at her. "It was that good for you?"

She couldn't contain her smile. "On a scale from one to ten, I'd give it a twenty. But that doesn't mean you should puff out your chest and tell the world what a master lover you are. Not until you give me everything."

"I will give you all you need, and more."

"Then do it."

"I prefer we retire to my bed."

"I prefer we not waste that much time."

"It is not about time or convenience," he said. "It is about protection."

Aha. The condom conversation. "I'm protected against pregnancy, and I have no communicable diseases."

"Nor do I. I receive a thorough physical every six months. Therefore, you do not have to concern yourself over that. If you trust me."

Darned if she didn't on this count, too. "I trust you."

"Good. You must know I would never do anything to put you in jeopardy."

But would he understand if she couldn't go through with it? Only one way to find out. "Then what are we waiting for?"

This time he took control, nudging her onto her back and centering his dark gaze on her. "Rest assured, I am weary of waiting. Are you certain you would not rather be lying on a proper mattress?"

"I'm only sure of one thing. If you don't make love to me now, I'm going to start pouting."

He kissed her softly before presenting her with one heck of a smoldering look. "I certainly do not wish to prolong your agony."

Then he kissed her again, touched her again, bringing her to the brink of another climax and a place where the past no longer existed. But when he parted her legs and moved atop her, that past came back to roost. She couldn't breathe, couldn't divorce herself from the memories of another cruel man, no matter how hard she tried. And regardless of the consequences, she jerked from beneath him and practically shouted, "Stop!"

Shaking and ashamed, Sunny sat up and hugged her knees to her chest. She waited for a few moments of silence to pass before explaining. "The same thing happened the one and only time Cameron tried to make love to me after the abduction. He left the next morning, and I never saw him again. I wouldn't blame you if you did the same thing."

"I am not your former lover, Sunny," he said. "I would not abandon you in your time of need, nor do I expect you to do something you are not able to do."

She shifted slightly to see his forearm draped over his eyes. "But I want to make love with you, Rayad. I've thought about nothing else since you said we'd be spending time outdoors. You were answering my greatest fantasy. I can't imagine going through the rest of my life not being a whole woman again. I just don't know how to get past this."

He rolled to his side and centered his gaze on her. "With my help, if you are willing. Yet you must be aware that if we never consummate our relationship, I will always respect you and fondly remember our time together."

Her heart executed a little leap in her chest. "I really want to try, but it could take time and a whole lot of patience."

"We have nothing better to do for the next few days."

"True."

He pushed off the blanket, came to his feet and offered his hand. "Now we will retire to bed where I will expect nothing more than to hold you while you sleep. Perhaps this one night I will chase away the night-mares."

He had a knack for saying all the right things. "That sounds like a good plan. I'd suggest we sleep here, but I don't want to wake up covered in sand with a sunburn."

When she tried to gather her clothes, he said, "Leave them here, and we will retrieve them tomorrow. I want you lying next to me naked."

She smiled at his demanding tone. "All right. As long as you're naked, too."

"I have no intention of wearing clothes this evening."

Sunny followed Rayad down the dimly lit stairs and into his private quarters. After they were securely set-tled into bed, he brought her into his arms, where she laid her cheek on his chest and listened to the beat of his strong heart. He rubbed her arm in a steady, sooth-ing rhythm, bringing about a welcome sense of peace.

She felt the need to express her appreciation for his patience and understanding, yet the right words escaped her. She found that odd considering her occupation re-volved around proper vocabulary. But that terminology dealt with facts, not emotions. Right then her emotions were running the gamut between gratitude and much deeper feelings.

Rather than tell him exactly what was in her heart, she chose something much less heavy. "You are a won-derful man, Rayad."

He softly kissed her forehead. "You are a remark-able woman, Sunny."

He made her feel remarkable. He made her trust she could finally conquer her fears and forget the terrible ordeal. Most important, he made her believe she could finally love a man the way she should. That she could truly love him.

Eight

He had never seen any woman look quite so innocent in sleep. He could not recall feeling such a fierce need to protect someone he had known such a limited amount of time. He found the unfamiliar emotions unwelcome and inadvisable. He must show restraint and be patient. He must allow her to signal him when she was ready to proceed with their intimacy. Above all, he had to accept that she could possibly reconsider.

Needing to leave her before he forgot his vow of restraint, Rayad moved his arm from beneath Sunny to gather what he needed to bathe, and afterward, swim. He sought an activity to expend energy and allow his body to calm.

After he retrieved the soap safe enough to use in the reservoir, he set the bar on the edge then dove into the pool. The water was much colder than usual, probably due to the current mountain storms that replenished the spring. Cold would serve him well, or so he thought as he returned to the ledge to begin his morning bath. No amount of frigid water would rid him of his need, he realized, when he glanced up to see Sunny standing on the stone bank, completely nude. The shape of her breasts, the curve of her hip and the slight shading between her thighs brought about another strong erection that he suspected would not disappear in the immediate future without tending.

She removed the band securing the now-misshapen braid, shook out her hair, stepped down into the water and walked toward him. "Good morning, kind sir," she said when she reached him.

He kept his hands fisted at his sides, though he longed to touch her. Everywhere. "Did you sleep well?"

"Better than I have in a long time." She looked up at the opening in the cave's ceiling before returning her gaze to his. "It's barely light outside. You must be an early riser."

She had no idea the accuracy in her assessment, yet she would if she came any closer. "I do not wish to waste the day by sleeping too long."

"I feel the same way, but I really have to take a shower to help me wake up."

"No need. I have everything here to accommodate your bath."

She tapped her chin with a fingertip. "That's right. This is your own personal tub."

"It is."

"You use soap?"

He nodded toward the bar on the bank. "I do. It is all natural and biodegradable. A woman in the village makes it especially for me."

She raised a thin brow. "Is that all she does for you?"

"She's almost eighty years of age."

"Oh. Mind if I inspect this soap?"

He would rather she inspect him. "Be my guest."

After she retrieved the bar, she came back to him and held it to her nose. "This smells fantastic, and it explains why you smelled so good last night."

"Do you wish to try it?"

"Unless you'd like to go first."

"I will wait until you are finished."

She took a few steps back and paused on the incline to where her torso was completely exposed. While he watched, she ran the soap over her arms, then her neck and finally her breasts, where she lingered longer than necessary. He decided she was bent on enticing him, and her ploy happened to be working. By the time she moved the bar down her abdomen, then beneath the water, he perched precariously on the edge of losing control.

"Mind washing my back?" she asked as she offered him the soap.

He did not mind, but he was not certain he would want to stop there. "As you wish."

After she turned away from him, he complied with her request, taking his time lathering her silky flesh while keeping a safe berth between them. Yet carnal urges began to commandeer his common sense as he traveled down to her well-shaped buttocks. And when she moved back and positioned herself flush against him, contacting the evidence of his lack of control, all his determination to resist her floated away with the bar of soap.

Without warning, he turned her around and kissed her with all the passion he experienced at that moment. He wanted to make her yearn more than any man she had ever yearned before. He desired to make her body weep for him with the highest form of intimacy possible, and he would—if she granted him permission. "I want to bring you to climax."

"I'm almost already there," she said, her voice a breathy whisper. "But I need you to finish me."

With that goal in mind, Rayad swept Sunny into his arms, set her on the edge of the bank and took his place between her parted legs. He pressed a line of kisses on her belly, careful to watch her face for any signs of distress before moving lower. Instead of issuing a protest, she leaned back using her elbows for support, closed her eyes and spread her legs wider. That was all the permission he needed to proceed.

He began by divining her flesh with his tongue then used strokes to bring her to completion, softer yet insistent. Even when he heard the increase in her respiration and sensed her impending orgasm, he did not let up. He tried to urge every sensation from her, and give her an experience that she would not soon forget.

After a few more moments, Sunny released a low moan and then bowed over his head, her entire body trembling. "That was incredible," she muttered before straightening to level her gaze on his. "And this is totally unfair to you."

He left the water to sit beside her. "I will manage."

She sent a pointed look at his groin. "All signs to the contrary."

"I have been without relief for extended periods of time."

She rose to her feet. "That ends now. Find me a towel and meet me in bed. And please don't argue. I want this to happen."

He wanted her more than she could ever know. Yet he must remember she might not be able to see their lovemaking through. "We do not need a towel," he said as he stood. "The sheets will dry."

She climbed into bed with a smile then beckoned him with open arms. They kissed for some time before she broke the contact and straightened, hovering above him. "I've decided I need to be on top," she announced, taking him by surprise.

"That would possibly be favorable for you." And undeniable pleasure for him.

"You have to promise me something first, Rayad."

"Anything you ask."

"Keep your eyes open and look at me the whole time. I need to see your face and know it's you."

"That will be my pleasure."

And it was, he determined, the moment she straddled his thighs and guided him inside her. He gritted his teeth against the need for immediate release when she began to move her hips, slowly at first then faster, taking him deeper and deeper. All the while, he kept

focused on her eyes though he found that task difficult in light of his imminent climax. He mustered all
his strength to hold back yet could no longer when she
leaned down and whispered, "I want to feel you let go."

The orgasm arrived with the force of a grenade, bind-
ing every muscle in his body. The pulsation went on
for longer than he had expected, or experienced to this
point in his checkered sexual history. In the time it took
for him to catch his breath, Sunny eased off him and
curled close to his side.

"You have to feel better."

He frowned. "Better does not appropriately describe
how I feel. The question is, how do you feel?"

She rolled onto her back and laughed. "Exhilarated.
Free. Like I just won a Pulitzer."

Her joy was contagious, bringing about his smile. "I
am glad. I have always been convinced you have the
strength of character to overcome this."

She turned her face toward him and formed her hand
around his jaw. "I'm not sure I would have, had it not
been for you. There is just one more thing I need from
you."

He hoped it had nothing to do with his dying devo-
tion or a declaration of love. He was too broken to give
her that. "I am listening."

"If at all possible, I want to use the radio."

He experienced a strong sense of relief. "To confirm
that I am not holding you here without good cause?"

She whisked a kiss across his chin. "I know you
haven't been lying about the storms. I just need to check
in with my sister."

He needed to take her features to memory for in a very short time, memories of this special woman would be all he had left. As it had been with the other remarkable woman who had once graced his life. "I will be glad to honor your request to speak with Piper. Perhaps it would be best if you do not tell her too much about our time here. I do not wish to explain to her husband."

Sunny favored him with a smile. "Don't worry. I'll pretend I'm having a terribly boring time."

"Having fun, Sunshine?"

She was speaking into a shortwave radio with a gorgeous man's-man standing behind her, running his hands up her T-shirt. She defined that as great fun. "So-so. Not much to do here."

"Where exactly is here?"

"South of Bajul."

"Adan said you were staying in a village."

"Not far from a village," she said, trying hard not to gasp as Rayad cupped her breasts. "Is it still raining there?"

"Unfortunately, yes, and it's not going to let up for at least another two days. What's the weather like there?"

"Hot." Extremely hot, and growing hotter by the minute. "How is Maysa?"

"Still pregnant, but she said she's been having some twinges, whatever that means. I hope you make it back before the big event."

She hoped her legs would hold her when Rayad unbuttoned her shorts. "Well, I just wanted to check in and see…" Her voice betrayed her when he slid the zipper down. "I just need…" To stop talking altogether.

"Sunny, are you there?"

Two more minutes and she would be. "Gotta go, sis. Bad connection. See you soon. Take care."

After she flipped the radio off, she turned into Rayad's arms and groaned. "You're determined to be a bad boy, aren't you?"

He nuzzled her neck then kissed her quick. "I know what I want, and I want you. Now."

She glanced behind her and realized the long table holding the communication equipment happened to be the only surface available. "You're not serious."

"Not here."

That gave her some relief. "Then where?"

"A place where I can finally fulfill one of your fantasies."

Her mental lightbulb snapped on. "Where we dined last night?"

"Yes."

"But it's still daylight."

He clasped her hand and brought it to his lips. "There is an erotic quality to spontaneity. Making love in the open and the possibility of detection only heightens that eroticism. However, it is highly unlikely anyone will come upon us since the perimeter is secure, if that is your concern."

She thought of one particular disconcerting scenario. "What about airplanes overhead?"

"Unless we are visited by Adan, that will not be an issue."

Great. Just what she needed—getting caught with her pants down by her brother-in-law. Time to put on the big-girl panties and get with the program. Or take them off as the case might be. "Well, no risk, no reward. Let's go."

Rayad led her back up the narrow steps and to the place where their journey to intimacy had begun. Once they arrived, Sunny discovered a different blanket spread out on the sand, and realized her new lover had planned this all along.

"Spontaneity, huh?" she said as she dropped down onto the makeshift bed.

He joined her and smiled—a sly one. "Perhaps not completely spontaneous, yet I did not know if you would agree."

He had a point. "I'll hand you that. What now?"

"Stand and take off your clothes."

"You don't want to do it?"

"I wish to watch."

His words generated more heat than the afternoon sun beating down on them. "I suppose I can do that since you've basically seen every part of me."

After returning to her feet, she crossed her arms and quickly pulled the T-shirt over her head, exposing her bare breasts. She tackled the rest of her clothing a bit slower in an effort to draw out the tension. Rayad visually followed her every move as she unfastened her shorts and let them fall to her feet, leaving her wearing the white muslin underwear.

"Satisfied?" she asked, even knowing what he would say.

"Everything, Sunny," he replied, confirming her prediction.

She shimmied out of the final garment and remained planted in the same spot, letting him look his fill. "Better?"

"Much better. Now come here."

"Not until you get naked, too."

Without hesitating, or standing, he began to strip but much faster than she had. Once he was down to his birthday suit, she reclaimed her place next to him. "You're leading this parade, so tell me what you want." And hopefully, she could deliver.

"Roll to your side away from me."

She threaded her lip between her bottom teeth. "I guess I could, but—"

"Do you trust me, Sunny?" he asked.

"Yes, I do."

"Then you must trust I will treat you with the greatest care. Now turn over and allow me to give you great pleasure."

Sunny complied and waited for what would come next, all the while thinking a month ago, she would never even consider doing this in the great outdoors. A month ago, she didn't know him. She was dizzy with anticipation. High on adrenaline and heated from head to toe.

He moved against her back, brushed her hair aside and whispered, "You will feel me better this way." Then he slid his leg between her legs, placed one hand between her thighs, and eased inside her.

Rayad had been right. The position allowed her to feel every nuance as he moved deep inside her. He began to stroke her with a fingertip, coaxing a climax that wouldn't take long at all. And it didn't.

Before she knew it—before she was ready—Sunny experienced an incredible orgasm made more powerful by Rayad's thrusts. She had truly found a paradise with him, and in turn rediscovered her natural sensuality.

Not long after, Rayad tensed against her, moved deeper inside her and released a low groan. He shuddered and when he climaxed, Sunny enjoyed every pleasant pulse of his body, knowing she'd given him as much pleasure as he had given her.

After a time, he loosened his hold on her and brought his lips to her ear. "Do you have any regrets?"

Only one. She turned into his arms and stroked his cheeks. "No regrets at all other than I hate this will all have to come to an end in the not-so-distant future. Unless you invite me to stay here indefinitely." When his expression went somber, she added, "Don't look so worried. I'm not serious, and I'm not going to start spewing sonnets and propose marriage. I know this is only temporary. When we leave here, you'll go back to your life, and I'll go back to mine."

"For that reason, I prefer we enjoy each other while we still have time."

Too little time to suit her, and that thought gave her pause. "I'm absolutely enjoying our time together now. You certainly know how to make a woman's fantasy come true."

He brushed her hair back from her face and lightly kissed her. "I vow to you I will endeavor to make each of your fantasies a reality in the days to come."

* * *

For three whole days, Rayad made good on his promise. He had touched her in every way possible and in places she didn't know existed. He had made love to her in various ways, with the exception of one due to his concern over her fear of confinement. He had been careful and considerate and extremely sexy. So sexy that he could have her with only a look, and he had several times.

Never before had she made love four times in twenty-four hours until she'd met him. Never before had she given that concept much thought. Cameron had been a once-a-week kind of guy. Her first lover had been an inexperienced jerk, but then they'd only been seventeen. Though her sexual conquests were somewhat limited, she knew enough to know that Rayad Rostam was a special breed. The kind of man who could steal a woman's heart like a thief in the night then leave with his own heart still intact.

Regardless of the possible emotional fallout, with every interesting conversation over shared meals, with every sultry kiss, every sweet nothing whispered in her ear, Sunny acknowledged she was in grave danger of losing herself to him and landing in love. Unfortunately, the danger had become her reality, and she'd already crashed and would probably burn from their inevitable parting.

She'd always been upfront to a fault, yet in this case she worried if she divulged her feelings to Rayad, he wouldn't reciprocate. She debated whether to come clean, or carry the secret the rest of her life. She despised secrets, and for that reason she decided to put it out in the open, let the chips fall and all that jazz.

On that thought, Sunny turned over in bed to find Rayad had left without her knowledge. She sat up and looked around, hoping to discover he'd gone for his morning bath and swim without her, though she would be disappointed if he had. The reservoir was undisturbed and the cavern starkly silent.

She needed to find him and confess before she lost her courage. That need drove her to search for her underwear balled up beneath the sheet at the end of the bed and put them on. Then she grabbed her discarded T-shirt and slipped it on while heading toward the bunker's entry.

When she stepped into the corridor, she heard Rayad's familiar voice, but she couldn't understand the Arabic he was speaking. She did detect a hint of anger in his tone. As soon as the conversation ended, she padded on bare feet to the radio room and peeked inside to see Rayad leaning back against the table, staring off into space.

"May I come in?" she asked.

"You may," he responded, although the stern look he gave her said she might not be welcome.

She didn't let that hinder her forward progress, or deter her from her goal. But before she started playing true confession, she would find out the reason behind his dark mood. "Were you chatting with anyone interesting?"

"Adan."

She moved to his side and hoisted herself up onto the desk. "What did he have to say?"

"Nothing that I wished to hear."

Getting information from him was like pulling hen's teeth, as her nana used to say. "I don't mean to intrude, but do you mind telling me what Adan told you that has you so cranky?"

"It does not involve you."

Cranky had become a colossal understatement. "Fine. It's probably something top secret that wouldn't interest me anyway." When he didn't respond, she determined a subject switch was in order. "I was thinking that after we bathe and have breakfast, we could go to the village a little earlier today. I saw a scarf I'd like to buy for Piper."

"That is not possible."

"I promise I'll pay you back."

He exhaled a rough sigh. "It is not possible to travel to the village, nor is it necessary."

Sunny could guess what he would say to her next question, and it made her heartsick to ask. But she had to know. "We have to leave, don't we?"

"Yes. I have been ordered to return to my duties immediately."

"What about the roads?"

"They were cleared as of yesterday."

She should be grateful he hadn't come by that information earlier, otherwise they would have missed out on several wonderful experiences. "I suppose that's good news."

"I suppose," he repeated, no clear emotion in his tone, only detachment.

Sunny felt as if he had erected a steel wall, effectively shutting her out. She refused to let him. "Look, we both knew this was going to happen, and maybe it's for the best. If we stayed together any longer, I would only…" Her determination to own up to her feelings trailed off along with her words.

Finally, he looked at her straight on. "You would only what?"

The moment had arrived to lay her heart on the line and hope it didn't get crushed. "I would only fall deeper in love with you."

He pushed off the table, laced his hands behind his neck and turned his back on her. "You cannot love me."

She wasn't at all surprised by his reaction, just the force of his demand. "I can, and I do. Believe me, this wasn't at all what I had planned, and it's ridiculous to think it happened this quickly. But I can't help the way I feel."

He faced her again, frustration reflecting in his dark eyes. "I cannot return your feelings. I will not allow it."

Allow it? "Why is that, Rayad? Because you enjoy being alone, or are you afraid of being vulnerable?"

"My fear would be for your emotional and physical safety. You are grateful for the attention I have given you, but you do not know me as well as you might think."

That made no sense whatsoever. "Unless you're some kind of ax murderer, I'm fairly sure I'm in no physical danger. And emotionally speaking, if you're intimating that I'm mistaking gratitude for love, you couldn't be more wrong. I know what it means to care that deeply for someone although I have to admit, I've never felt this strongly for anyone. Maybe you've never experienced that before, and if that's true, I feel sorry for you."

"This has nothing to do with my previous experience," he said. "If I continued an affair with you, I could be putting you in jeopardy."

Affair—that about said it all. "Is this because of your military ties?"

"That is partially true."

Just when she thought she was beginning to solve the puzzle, he introduced another piece. "What do you mean *partially*?"

"Leave it be, Sunny. There are things you do not want to know."

She hopped off the desk and moved in front of him. "I want to know everything about you, Rayad. I mistakenly believed I did. You definitely know everything about me, including details about the abduction I've never told anyone. It's only fair you return the favor by telling me what you've been hiding."

Indecision warred in his eyes before he returned to his stoic persona. "I do not dare tell you all there is to tell. I have already risked being tried for treason for breaching security by bringing you here. Rafiq would not object, but if the governing council knew, I could be hanged."

That was news to her. Distressing news. "And you're just now telling me this?"

"I felt it was worth the risk. You needed a respite in a place where you could heal."

Every moment they'd made love now somehow seemed false. "Thanks bunches for being my sheikh in shining armor, but here's a newsflash. I don't need to be rescued. I do need to know that when you made love to me, it meant something other than my consolation prize for being your bed buddy the past few days."

"You are not being reasonable. You knew this arrangement would only be short-term."

Every bitter emotion crowded in her at once, and if she didn't leave, she might actually cry. "Yes, I did know it wasn't going to be forever. I didn't know I'd be foolish enough to fall for your charms and mistake you for a decent guy capable of real emotions. And I'm really sorry I did. I'll go pack my things now."

When she started away, Rayad clasped her arm, preventing her from making a hasty exit. "I wish I could tell why it is not possible for us to be together," he said when she faced him. "But I cannot."

"Yes, you can. You owe me that much."

He hesitated as if he might have begun to waffle. "It is classified information."

She'd decided to give it another shot, and to make it a good one. "I really don't care about your government secrets, nor should you after what we've shared. You know that whatever you say will go no further than this room."

"You will never see me in the same light, and I would prefer we part while you still believe I am a man of honor."

Her belly tightened at the thought of what he could have done to make him believe she would toss him away like yesterday's trash. Her mind began to reel with the possibilities. He was a military man, and that position at times required many things, the least of which was violence. Still… "You said you're involved in intelligence. I always gathered that meant investigating insurgents and other covert activities."

"It does, but my duties go beyond that realm. They have for some time now."

Finally, she was getting somewhere. She just wasn't sure she would like where they were going. "If you're trying to protect me from the fact that you've killed someone, that's not necessary. I know the realities of warfare, and I understand that soldiers don't always have a choice. It's either kill or be killed. If that's the case with you, then I promise I won't think less of you."

A muscle ticked in his tightened jaw. "Again I implore you to leave it be, Sunny."

She couldn't leave it be, not until she had answers. Not until she quieted the warning bells in her head. "Tell me what you're hiding, or I'll walk out of here without you right this minute, even if I have to travel back to the palace on foot."

Turning his attention to some unknown focal point, Rayad remained silent for several excruciating moments. Sunny's heart began to beat faster while she waited for him to finally look her in the eye.

"I have always had a choice."

Her mind grew foggy with confusion. "I don't understand."

"If you must know everything, then I will tell you."
She witnessed a flash of remorse in his eyes, then an
intensity that shook her to the core as he said, "I have
been trained to kill."

Nine

"You're an assassin?"

The indictment in Sunny's query had an unexpected impact on Rayad. He wanted and needed her respect, which would require details, no matter the consequences. "Trust me when I tell you my duty is necessary."

"Trust you?" She released a humorless laugh. "I'm standing in a cave with a man who intentionally shoots to kill. I slept with a killer. Forgive me if I find that a bit disturbing."

He moved forward, and when she backed away, he felt as if she had run him through with a blade. "Do you understand that if I wanted to harm you, I would have already done so?"

She seemed to mull that over for a moment. "This

isn't about me. It's about what you do. I can't begin to imagine intentionally taking someone's life."

She could not imagine the monsters he had seen. "Would you feel more comfortable if I told you my services have rarely been needed?"

"Exactly how many have there been?"

If he told her, he'd been further crossing into treacherous territory, and not because of the minimal incidents. "I pledged my loyalty and silence when I assumed my military obligation. Any admission would be a direct betrayal to my country."

"Failure to admit it will only make me worry about my judgment when it comes to men."

He despised that she would doubt herself, or his intentions. Therefore, he would supply the answers she needed. "Two men. One had been plotting to set off a bomb in the middle of the village at the behest of a radical coalition based north of Bajul. The other planned to gun down Rafiq's father during a public event. I was charged with protecting the former king."

"I see. The assassin destroyed the assassin. Makes perfect sense." The cynicism in her voice said otherwise.

"As difficult as it might be for you to believe, I was forced into this position." Now that he had revealed too much, he braced for more questions.

"Explain how someone is forced to become a killer."

He was torn between remaining silent and telling her the entire truth. To return to that part of his past would be painful, and he hated to resurrect those long-buried emotions. To refuse the woman who had boldly admitted her love for him would be unforgivable.

Rather than search for the words, he chose to show her. "If you want answers, then you must come with me to a place where you will find them."

She folded her arms beneath her breasts. "Before I agree to do this, you have to give me more information about where you are taking me."

The fact he had destroyed her trust wounded him deeply. "It is a site in the desert not far from here." He looked down at her bare feet. "Our hike will require appropriate shoes."

"I don't care if I have to don a parka and knee boots, as long as I can solve this mystery."

"As soon as you dress, I will meet you at the entry of the bunker."

"Fine. I won't be long."

After Sunny departed, Rayad questioned his wisdom, and if he would be able to provide all the information she needed to understand why he had lost his soul, and his way. Why his heart had been broken beyond repair. Why he could never be the man she needed.

The sweltering heat began to take its toll on Sunny as they trekked through several passages on rocky ground. After twenty minutes of unsuccessfully trying to keep up with her guide, she rounded one giant stone formation and entered open desert. She caught sight of Rayad standing atop a dune and headed toward him to see why he had stopped. Hopefully, they'd arrived at their destination, though she saw nothing other than desolate terrain devoid of all forms of life. But when she climbed the sand hill and came to his side, she viewed a veritable oasis in the middle of nowhere, with an olive grove on one side, along with palm trees and varied plants on the other. In the middle of all the unexpected greenery, another sight sent shockwaves coursing through her. A massive pile of stone and charred wood, soaring to at least thirty feet, if not more, marred the inviting landscape.

"What is this place?" she asked, once she'd recovered enough to speak.

"The key to my past."

When Rayad began to stride toward the ruins, adrenaline gave Sunny a burst of energy, and she matched him step for step. He stopped at a tangled metal structure that appeared to have once been a gate and took a seat on what was left of the stone support.

She claimed the spot beside him and waited for further explanation. When it didn't come, she opted to prod him. "Tell me about this place and what happened here, Rayad."

"This was once my palace," he said with surprising detachment. "It was destroyed in an explosion."

She'd predicted a fire had caused its demise. Wasn't the first time she'd been wrong today. "Was anyone hurt?"

"Two of my staff members were killed, and there were others."

As much as she hated that innocent employees had lost their lives, the *others* greatly interested her. "Who else was here?"

"My wife and our three-year-old son."

She'd mistakenly believed she wouldn't be stunned anymore today. "You told me you'd never been married."

"I told you I was not presently married."

When she thought back to their initial conversation, she realized he was right. In fact, she recalled he'd evaded the question, and she'd sensed a story behind that evasion. Time to get to the bottom of that story. "This wasn't an accident, was it?" she asked, though she knew the answer.

"It was not."

Now everything had begun to become crystal clear, except for pertinent details. "Who did this?"

He momentarily covered his face with both hands before returning his attention to the destruction. "Some vengeful person who wished to strip me of all that I held dear."

At the sound of the abject sorrow in his voice, Sunny fought to hold back her own emotions. "I am so, so sorry, Rayad. I hope the perpetrator suffered for his acts."

He fisted his hands resting on his thighs. "I have never discovered the murderer's identity, though I have spent ten years searching for the evil miscreant who destroyed my home and my life."

"And this is what led you to become an assassin."

"Yes. I used my connections in an effort to root him out, and on the day I finally confront him, I will kill him on sight."

"What if that day never comes?"

"I will not stop searching until I find them, or draw my last breath. I owe that to my wife and child."

The quest for revenge had obviously consumed him for years, and still did. "I don't know anything about your wife, but if she was like most women, she wouldn't want you wasting your life on a futile mission to avenge her death."

Rayad stood and began to pace, hands knitted together behind his neck. "Lira was not like most women. She was kind and gentle and a superior mother. She worshipped our son, Layth, as well as myself."

At least now she had names to go with his family, and a strong sense of sympathy for his plight. "I can't imagine what you've had to endure, but I do hope that someday you'll try to be happy."

He kept pacing liked a caged cougar, as if he couldn't physically stand still without succumbing to the sorrow. He also avoided looking at her. "I cannot be happy until I avenge my family's deaths by destroying their killer."

"And if that happens, will you truly be content knowing you exchanged one life for another?"

"Four lives," he said adamantly as he turned toward her. "I will achieve some semblance of atonement for my transgressions. Had it not been for my duty, they would still be alive."

She pushed off the stone pillar and stood before him. "But you still have no idea who might be responsible."

"I have followed several leads, but all have been dead ends. I still have more to investigate, including enemies of my father."

Evidently, he was into self-torture. "Then you're saying this tragedy could have resulted from your father's connections, and you might not be responsible at all?"

He dropped his arms to his sides and looked defiant. "That possibility is remote at best. Regardless, I moved Lira and Layth to this remote location to protect them. I failed in that endeavor and by virtue of the fact I should have been there that night. My covert activities prevented me from achieving that goal."

"And if you'd been there, you would be dead, too."

"In the beginning I wished that very thing. My mission aided me in moving forward."

"You're not moving forward, Rayad. You're caught in a prison comprised of guilt and hatred."

His expression went stone cold. "Have you not wished ill will on your captors?"

"As a matter of fact, I have. I've fantasized about tying my abductor up in a heavy blanket and beating him with a baseball bat. My therapist said that was healthy, as long as I didn't act on it. I thought that was kind of humorous since I can't harm a phantom."

"And you have never desired to know his identity?"

"What would be the point? It's done, and it's over. The experience has made me more cautious and maybe a little fearful. But I'm determined to get over that rather than let the experience stifle me. Believe it or not, you helped me to see the importance in regaining my life. I'm sorry you can't seem to regain yours."

He turned his attention back to the monument of destruction. "We should return to the palace now. And again I remind you not to mention this to anyone. Very few people know about my past."

"Does that include my sister?"

"Yes. Adan is bound to his promise to me not to speak of it with anyone, including his wife."

"Don't worry," she said. "Your secrets are all safe with me. Good luck carrying them to your grave."

As she walked away, Sunny realized all too well that nothing she said to Rayad would ever break through his resolve to remain static in his life. If he chose to remain immersed in his grief and his search for retaliation, so be it.

He could never be the man for her, and that made her incredibly sad. Even worse, he would never let himself love again, and she couldn't save him from that fate. She wouldn't even try.

"Well?"

After a silent drive to the palace, and an uncomfortable family dinner, Sunny had retired to her suite to unpack and get some sleep. That plan had been thwarted by her sister, who now hovered over her like a mother hen. "Well what, Piper?"

"Did you enjoy your time with Rayad?"

Until today, she could confirm that had been the case. "It was nice while it lasted."

Piper sent her a suspicious look. "Did the two of you…you know."

Unfortunately, she did know what her twin was intimating and decided to throw her a bone. "Yes, we did *you know*. Several times. Are you happy now?"

"Question is, Sunny, are you happy? I'm thinking the answer is no."

She tossed the last of her clothes onto the bureau and her tote in a nearby chair. "Look, we had a good time, it was great, but it's over. End of story."

Piper perched on the edge of the mattress and stared like a hawk scoping out its prey. "If he did something to hurt you, tell me, and I'll have Adan deal with him."

Sunny shoved the bag aside and practically collapsed into the chair. "He didn't do anything to hurt me, so I don't need you to ask your husband to beat him up. We're both adults, and we knew whatever transpired was only temporary. Now if you don't mind, it's late, and I'd like to get to bed."

Her sister put on a stellar pout and pushed up from the bed. "Okay. I know when I'm not wanted. But I want all the dirty details before you leave in two weeks, even if I have to force you to talk."

As much as she hated to drop a bad news bomb, Sunny felt she had no choice. "On that subject," she began as she stood, "I'm probably going to leave in a couple of days. I'm ready to get back to work."

"We've barely had time to talk, Sunny. Won't you reconsider staying at least a week?"

She might if she didn't have to face Rayad on a daily basis. Then again, he could be leaving shortly to return to his mission of death and destruction. "I'll think about it as soon as I get a good night's sleep."

Piper came to her feet. "Fine. I'll leave as soon as you answer one more question."

Great. Just great. "Make it quick."

"Where exactly did you stay?"

In a mystical cavern in the company of a mysterious,

tortured, gorgeous man. "Some primitive place near a small village."

"No room service?"

She'd been serviced, and often. "Definitely not. There was only one bed, but it was decent."

"I'm surprised you even noticed the bed when you had a hunk occupying it with you. If he's anything like Adan, you didn't even need a bed."

With that, Piper grinned and rushed out of the room before Sunny could launch a verbal retaliation.

Weary and worn out, Sunny took her second shower of the day, brushed her teeth and hair, dressed in her favorite blue silk sleep shirt and slipped beneath the covers. Her mind wouldn't seem to shut off and allow her to sleep, so she turned on the bedside lamp and attempted to read the mystery novel she'd brought with her. She couldn't concentrate, thanks to the mental slideshow featuring wonderful moments with Rayad. At times the recollections caused her face to flush, and other memories made her heartsick. At least an hour passed before she finally gave in to the lure of sleep.

"I need you…"

Sunny came awake with a start, at first believing she'd been dreaming. But as her vision came into focus, she saw her dream man standing next to the bed, dressed in only a pair of navy pajama bottoms. "What are you doing here?"

"I need to be next to you one last night, though I know I do not deserve it."

He looked so lost and forlorn, she scooted over and lifted the covers. "Okay, but just so you know, we're only going to sleep."

"I understand," he said as he slid into the bed beside her.

As he stacked his hands behind his head, she rolled to her side to face him. "Too much on your mind to rest?" she asked, breaking the silence.

"Yes."

"I had the same problem. I'd just drifted off right before you arrived."

"My apologies for waking you." He sent her a fast glance before going back to inspecting the ceiling. "If you wish me to leave, I will do so."

"I *wish* you would talk to me, Rayad. Let me in, and let me know what you're thinking."

He exhaled a rough sigh. "It would be too difficult."

"It would be cathartic."

When he failed to respond, Sunny assumed he was bent on ignoring her suggestion. Then suddenly he said, "My code name is Lion."

She hadn't expected that revelation. "Okay. Why are you telling me this now?"

"Layth means lion. I took it in honor of my son."

She inched closer to his side, drawn to his undeniable grief. "Did the name suit him as well as it does you?"

His ensuing smile looked so very sad. "It did. He was a very brave boy. Highly intelligent. Always in motion and into trouble at times. Yet he had a very caring side to him. He inherited that from his mother."

"He inherited some of that from you."

The comment drew his gaze. "How can you believe that when you know who I am and what I am capable of doing?"

She wanted to scream from frustration. "It's not fundamentally who you are, Rayad. It's a bitter force that drives you to try to be that man. You'll never be able to succeed because believe it or not, there's still too much good in you."

"I am beyond redemption," he said as he reached over and snapped off the light.

Against better judgment, Sunny settled her cheek on his chest. "You're so very wrong. It's obvious you loved your wife, and I suspect she loved you, too."

"You are correct. I loved her the first time I set eyes on her."

On one hand, Sunny wasn't sure she wanted to know all the details. On the other, she had the opportunity to finally glimpse the real man behind the steely exterior. "When did the two of you meet?"

"The night our fathers announced our betrothal."

Incredible. An arranged marriage that had gone right, until fate took a wrong turn. "How old were you when you married?"

"I was nineteen, and she had barely turned eighteen. Layth was born two years later. That was the most monumental day of my life." He paused and drew in a breath before continuing. "I remember how it felt the first time I held my son in my arms. I recall his first smile and the day he took his first steps when I returned from a month-long mission. For many years I have rejected those memories, but lately I cannot."

"You shouldn't deny them, Rayad. Letting yourself remember will help you finally heal."

"The loss has left a wound in my soul that will never heal."

"Have you ever cried for them?" she asked.

"No. I feared if I did, I would never stop. No man should live long enough to bury his beloved wife and child."

The slight break in his voice made Sunny want to cry for him. Instead, she moved closer and held him tighter. They stayed that way for a long time, until Rayad pulled her to him and kissed her with all the passion she had come to know in his arms. Before long, they were naked and touching each other without restraint. And when it came time to consummate their temporary, troubled union one final time, Sunny let go of her own fears and pulled him on top of her. She relished his weight, the closeness of his powerful body as he moved inside her. She welcomed her climax and loved the way he said her name when he found his own release. She loved him, period, with all her heart and soul.

In the aftermath, Rayad was so still, she thought he'd fallen asleep. But then he shifted back beside her, draped his arm across her abdomen and laid his cheek against her shoulder. That's when she felt the dampness on her flesh. That's when she knew he had finally given in to the tears that were long overdue. That's when she started to hope that maybe, just maybe, the healing had truly begun.

"Wake up, Sunshine. It's happening!"

Sunny pried her eyes open, glanced at Piper then remembered Rayad's late-night visit. She turned her head to see only an empty space beside her, and for once she appreciated his habit of sneaking off without waking her.

She sat up against the headboard and yawned. "Okay, Pookie. What's got your drawers in a wad this morning?"

"Maysa's in labor. Actually, she's been in labor all night. The doctor says it should be any time now."

"Why aren't you at the hospital?"

Piper rolled her eyes. "She's not in the hospital. She's in her suite. Apparently, tradition dictates that a future king is born at the palace, barring any emergency."

Of all the archaic practices, this had to top the list. "What if she has to have a C-section?"

Piper plopped down on the end of the bed. "According to Rafiq, they've prepared for that and have a makeshift operating room set up in the basement and an ambulance standing by. But it looks like she's going to deliver without any problems."

Sunny threw the covers aside, thankful she'd put on a T-shirt last night, and that she didn't find any obvious evidence of Rayad's presence. "I'll take a quick shower and join you."

"Meet me upstairs in the family sitting room," Piper said on her way to the door. "But hurry. I want you to be there when they bring the baby out. No one knows if it's a boy or a girl."

"I bet it's one or the other," Sunny called to her sister, but the snide comment clearly feel on deaf ears.

As much as she liked Rafiq and Maysa, she wasn't in the mood to celebrate a birth. But the prospect of seeing Rayad again drove her from the bed to complete her morning routine. Provided he actually showed up.

He did not want to be there, yet family loyalty overrode his wants and desires. He had been watching the clock for well over an hour, when he had not been thinking about his night with Sunny.

As if those memories had come to life, she appeared in the doorway, dressed in the flowing blue caftan he had purchased for her in the village and a pair of gold sandals. She looked as beautiful as she had the first time he had seen her standing beneath the palace portico. Her blond hair curled around her slender shoulders, bringing to mind the times he had kissed her there. He took a visual journey across her face, his gaze coming to rest on her lips to find her smile was absent. He was to blame for that, as well as the sadness in her eyes.

Following the lead of the rest of the men present in the room, Rayad came to his feet, battling the urge to go to her and kiss her soundly. For that reason, he thought it best to avoid her at all costs.

As unwelcome fate would have it, she crossed the room and claimed the chair next to his. "Did you finally get some sleep?" she asked with a smile.

"Some," he muttered. "And you?"

"Same here. Are you okay?"

He recognized the referral to his emotional breakdown, a subject he did not wish to broach. "I am ready to return to my duties."

"Of course you are."

The venom in her tone filled him with regret, and

the wish that he could be the man who would grant her every desire. An impossible undertaking.

When the conversation ceased, Rayad grabbed a magazine from the side table and pretended to read. The room remained abuzz with speculation over the child's gender, creating an atmosphere that hindered his concentration. Having Sunny so close did not help his predicament, either.

If only he could find an excuse to leave before the birth, yet that would be too obvious. If only the queen would get on with it.

"Ladies and gentlemen, may I have your attention please."

Rayad glanced up from the magazine to see the balding, bespectacled Deeb, the palace's executive assistant, standing in the entry. The man cleared his throat twice before he garnered everyone's attention.

"It is with great pride, and the parents' blessing, that I present to you Bajul's newest royal son, Prince Ahmed ibn Rafiq Mehdi."

A son. Rayad froze the moment Rafiq walked into the room, the infant cradled in his arms. All the memories he had tried so mightily to keep at bay came rushing in on him. The crowd gathered around the newborn thwarted any escape, and he realized Sunny was at the forefront of the celebration.

"May I hold him?" he heard her ask, and Rafiq granted her request, though Rayad found that odd since she was not a blood relative.

He also found it odd that she seemed to be approaching him, her gaze unwavering. He was completely astonished when she arrived and handed him the child. "This is what it's all about, Rayad. This new baby is a sign that life does go on even during the darkest of times."

He looked down on the sleeping child and remembered, not with bitterness and regret, but with wonder. He silently welcomed this boy into the world and prayed that no harm would ever come to him. Yet when the pain of remembrance became too great, he intended to hand him back to Sunny, and found her gone.

And there he stood, holding a child that was not his, and with little hope of ever having another.

Ten

Sunny wasn't surprised when Rayad stormed into the suite, primed for a confrontation. That had been her plan all along. A chance to implement Sunny's Last Stand.

"You had no right or cause to put me through such agony," he said, his voice teeming with fury.

She kept right on packing her toiletries, as if he'd told her he appreciated the gesture. "Like it or not, you needed a wake-up call."

He strode across the room and stood at the foot of the bed, hands fisted at his sides like he wanted to throw a punch. "That is not for you to decide."

She afforded him only a brief glance before resuming her preparation for departure. "Someone had to do it, Rayad, and it might as well be me."

"I resent your intrusion."

After zipping the carry-on, she calmly picked it up from the bench and then set it on the floor with the larger bag. Only then did she give him her full attention. "As of tomorrow, I'll be out of here and out of your life for good."

"Where are you going?"

Funny, he sounded almost disappointed. "Back to Atlanta then back to work."

"Why so soon?"

"I'd think that would be obvious. This palace isn't big enough for the both of us. As long as you're here, I can't get over you, and that is unacceptable. But before I go, I have a few things I need to say."

He took the chair in the corner, crossed his slack-covered legs like a gentleman, and said, "Please. Be my guest. That should allow me time to calm enough not to say something I will later regret."

She chose the bedpost spot that he'd recently vacated to give it her best effort before giving up. "First, I sincerely didn't mean to hurt you today by handing you the baby. I only wanted to force you to realize that life renews itself, if only you'll let it. My mistake."

He streaked a hand over his jaw. "We have been through this before."

"Secondly," she continued. "I love you, Rayad. More than you will ever know. But I won't stay another minute and watch you die inside a little more each day because you can't forgive yourself."

He uncrossed his legs and lowered his head. "I do not merit forgiveness."

She went to him, knelt down and laid her hands on

his thighs. "Yes, you do. And someday you'll wake up alone and realize you've missed out on a future full of happiness and love. Do you really want to face that, or would you rather spend your days with a woman who both loves and accepts you unconditionally?"

He took her hands, came to his feet while simultaneously pulling her into his arms. They embraced for several moments before he let her go and sought her eyes. "I do not understand what you see in me, Sunny, nor do I understand how you so readily accepted my many transgressions. I am honored to have met such a remarkable woman."

There it was—the inevitable goodbye. She refused to shed a tear, even though they threatened to make an appearance. She'd rather part on good terms and a smile, which she gave him. "I'm not so remarkable, Rayad. I'm just your average girl who hopes to one day find a guy who loves her like crazy."

"I wish that could be me. Since it cannot, I have no doubt you will find a man who better deserves you."

Hard for her to imagine that now that she'd found the best. Too bad he didn't realize it. "Thanks for the optimistic outlook on my future partner, and most important, for giving me back my confidence."

"It was always there, Sunny. You did not need my assistance, only minimal prodding. Rest assured I would not take back those moments with you, and our lovemaking meant more to me than you realize."

If she didn't get away from him now, she would have a total meltdown. In an effort to prevent that, Sunny headed to the desk in the corner, retrieved a piece of royal stationery, and jotted down her personal information. When she was done, she willed her composure to return before she went back to him and offered him the paper. "This is my temporary address until I find a new apartment, and my cell phone number. Should you happen to find yourself in Atlanta, stop by and see me. And if you change your mind and decide, miracle of all miracles, you want to give us a chance, give me a call. If you don't, call me anyway if you'd like, just so I know you're okay. That is, when you're not packing an AK-47 and searching for bad guys, of course." She attempted a smile, but she was sure it fell flat.

He stared at the page for a few moments before centering his gaze on hers. "I can make no promises."

"I know that," she said, her eyes beginning to mist. "Just promise me you'll at least try to be safe."

"I will try."

She gave in to her need to hold him again, and he thankfully accepted her embrace. He also gave her a gentle kiss that only served to shatter her heart a little more. Then he left without looking back, or saying goodbye.

After the door closed behind him, signifying the end to an unforgettable chapter in her life, Sunny stretched out across the bed and cried.

For seven long days she had been gone. For seven long nights he had missed her company.

Rayad could only think of one way to abandon all thoughts of Sunny McAdams and bring his mind back to the ever-present mission.

For that reason, he dressed in uniform and sought out his commander-in-chief. "I am respectfully requesting my immediate return to active duty, Adan."

His cousin did not bother to rise from the chair when he'd strode into the office without announcing his arrival. Nor did Adan look surprised by the request.

"The answer to that is no, Rayad. You have yet to be medically cleared."

"I am completely recovered."

"We'll see what the physician says about that."

Fortunately he had prepared for this argument. "I saw him earlier this morning and he pronounced me quite well. If you do not trust me, call him."

"I will most certainly do that," Adan said. "And then *I* will determine if I believe you are not only mentally but physically ready to return to work."

Rayad braced his hands on the desk and leaned forward. "If my memory serves me correctly, you summoned me back to the palace last week because you were in need of my services, yet you have avoided me since my return."

Adan tossed the pen he'd been gripping aside and watched it roll onto the floor. "I lied about the mission."

His blood began to boil over the deception. "Why?"

"Because of my concern for my sister-in-law's well-being."

"I did not harm her, nor would I."

"Not intentionally," Adan said. "But Piper believes you didn't help her, either. In fact, my wife is convinced you're the reason she departed earlier than planned."

He could deny that conjecture, but then he would

be telling a falsehood. "She is preparing to resume her career."

Adan inclined his head and studied him straight on. "Are you certain about that? Sunny seemed fairly down in the dumps when she left, not to mention I've been informed you took advantage of her during your respite."

One more insult, and they might come to blows, as they had a time or two in their youth. "No advantage was taken. Sunny and I are adults, and what transpired between us was consensual."

This time Adan leaned forward and glared at him. "I know you, Rayad. After your wife's death, you used your mysterious charm and machismo to pull women into your tangled web. Then you would leave them high and dry with a wounded heart."

He felt the need to defend himself, despite the truth in his cousin's acerbic comments. "What I shared with Sunny was very different. She is different. I care a great deal for her. More than I have cared for any woman in years. I would never intentionally cause her any pain, emotional or physical. Still, I am not the man for her, and that is why I was forced to let her go, although I despised every second of it."

Adan suddenly began to laugh. "Bloody hell, Rayad, you're in love with her."

He straightened from the shock of hearing his name in relationship to that word. "I did not say that."

"You didn't have to say it. It is written all over your lovesick face."

Rayad realized Adan was correct in his assumption. He had fallen in love with the beautiful journalist. He loved her still, and most likely always would love her. Yet one issue still prevented him from exploring their relationship further—he had yet to find those responsible for murdering his wife and child. "Regardless of my feelings, I cannot act on them."

Adan chose that moment to stand, sending the rolling chair backward into the bookshelf behind him. "Are you daft, Rayad? Of course you can act on them. Nothing is holding you here. You have more money than you can spend, and you no longer have a home to speak of. I will grant you an extended leave to get your head on straight and go after her, the same as I went after my wife. I have not once regretted that decision, and neither will you."

The suggestion seemed to make sense, yet he harbored several concerns. "I have not found my family's killers. She would never understand my need to complete that mission."

His cousin leaned forward and glared at him. "Perhaps it's time to move on from that mission."

Had Adan suggested that before Sunny, Rayad would have immediately rejected that notion. "If I did decide to seek her out, though I am not claiming I will, she most likely would refuse to see me."

"My bride also happened to tell me Sunny gave you her number and address," Adan said. "That is not the action of a woman who doesn't want to see you."

Another correct assessment, followed by more internal debate. "If I pursued a relationship with Sunny, I would be giving up all that I have gained in my career. I would be giving up on avenging my wife and child's deaths."

"And the gifts you would receive in return would be tenfold." Adan sighed. "Just remember, retaliation won't bring your wife and child back, Rayad. You should put the past to rest, otherwise, your futile quest will rob you of a future with Sunny. Honor your wife and son by learning to love again."

His cousin's logic only served to confuse him. "I will take your advice into consideration, but I make no promises."

"Fine, but don't wait too long to decide. And should you need to pay Sunny a visit, I will personally fly you to the States myself."

"In the meantime, I will report for duty at the base in the morning," he said as he walked away from his well-meaning cousin.

Rayad left the office in a state of turmoil. He could not go to Sunny unless he was prepared to discard his need for revenge. He could not give his all to her unless he learned to forgive himself. He could not move forward in his life unless he prepared to let go of the past.

Until he was absolutely certain he could manage all those things, he would return to his mission with only memories of a very special woman who had changed him in many ways through her unconditional acceptance. If that certainty did not come, he would face spending the rest of his days alone. And for the first time in many, many years, that concept no longer appealed to him.

He had much to decide and hoped he arrived at the correct decision. Only time would tell.

When the bell rang, Sunny was just about ready to give the pizza guy a good piece of her mind for taking two hours to deliver her dinner. Poised to do that very thing, she threw open the door, only to find not some skinny adolescent, but her erstwhile lover and favorite tough guy. She opened her mouth, closed it then opened it again. "Is this a mirage?"

He cracked a crooked smile. "No mirage. May I come in?"

"Of course. Have a seat and take a load off."

He sent her a confused look as he breezed past her then dropped down on the lounger next to the sofa. It took a minute for Sunny to move, and she was trembling so badly she thought she might shake right out of her fuzzy purple slippers.

After she sat down on the couch, she stared at him a moment, expecting him to disappear. "If I'd known you were coming, I would've baked cookies. Or at least dressed in something nicer than sweats and a hoodie."

"You look as beautiful as I remember."

So did he in his navy sport coat, matching slacks and white shirt. "Mind telling me why you're here?"

"I have been doing a lot of thinking since you left Bajul."

"About?"

"Us."

"And?"

He leaned forward, his hands clasped before his

parted knees, his usual position when he was about to get all serious. "I returned to duty for a few days, yet I could not stop remembering our time together. I could not discard that the danger I frequently face might take me away from you permanently."

I will not hope. I will not hope… "But we're not really together, Rayad."

"And that is why I am here." He hesitated a moment before he spoke again. "You have been right about many things, Sunny, the least of which involves my inability to regain my life. I want to change."

She leaned across the end table and touched his arm. "You can, Rayad. You will."

"I am still not certain that is true. I know I cannot accomplish that without your help, yet I question if it would be fair to ask that of you."

Hope crept back in despite her determination to stop it. "I can only help if you let me, and that's going to be difficult if you're determined to find your family's killer."

"I have taken a leave from the military, with Adan's blessing."

Once again she was shocked senseless. "Does Adan know about us?"

He leaned back and rubbed his chin. "He does. He was instrumental in convincing me to seek you out. He went so far as to pilot the plane that brought me to Atlanta once I decided to come here."

The next time she saw her brother-in-law, she was going to give him a big sisterly kiss. "I can only imagine that conversation."

"He told me that he regretted almost letting your sister go, but he doesn't regret seeking her out and making a life with her."

"It's obvious he doesn't."

His gaze drifted away before he leveled it on her again. "Would you be willing to return to Bajul with me?"

"Why would I do that when I just got back from there a month ago?"

"Because I wish to be with you."

"For how long?"

"Until we determine if we are suited for each other."

Not quite good enough, but close. "I can't throw away my career and run off with you on the chance that you might want to seriously pursue a relationship."

"You could still work and be based in Bajul."

Damn his logic. "That still doesn't diminish the risk I'd be taking, especially since you've never really said how you truly feel about me."

"Would you take that risk if I told you I love you?"

Exactly what she wanted to hear, but could she believe him? "How do you know you love me?"

He rose from the chair to join her on the sofa and wrapped one arm around her shoulder. "For the past few weeks, my nightmares have been replaced with dreams of you, when I happened to actually sleep. You are all I have thought about, and the ache over the loss of you has been unbearable. I know I do not deserve your forgiveness for my disregard, but I implore you—"

"Shut up and kiss me, Rayad."

He did as she asked, melding his lips to hers in a meaningful, heartfelt kiss.

Once they parted, she asked the question foremost on her mind. "If I do decide to return with you, where will we stay?"

"That is a dilemma. I would offer the cavern, but it will soon be filled with military trainees. Perhaps I should stay here for a time. I have seen little of the United States, and I have never explored Georgia."

"That sounds just peachy," she said, even knowing the Southern reference would be lost on him. "Do you honestly believe we can make this work after knowing each other such a short time?"

"Do you still love me?"

She laid her head on his shoulder. "Yes, I do."

"Will you always accept my faults and failures?"

"If you'll accept mine."

"Then I do believe we have a chance at a bright future."

"So do I." And she did.

"Someday I hope to have another child."

Only then did she know for sure he was ready to move on. "I'd like to have children, too, at some point in time."

"I am happy to hear that. And in the very near future, you should know I plan make you my bride."

She reared back and stared at him. "Hold your horses, Arabian cowboy. Let's slow down a bit. First we need to get each to know each other better before we even consider going down that road."

He pressed a kiss on her cheek. "I agree, yet I will

warn you I am not always a patient man, and I can be very persuasive."

"That might be true," she said. "But it's going to take more than pretty words and a lot of good sex to convince me we need to get married anytime soon."

He gave her a wink and a patently sexy smile. "We shall see."

She winked back. "Yes, we will."

"By the power vested in me by the great state of Georgia, I now pronounce you husband and wife."

And there, a scant three months later, while standing on the lawn of a gorgeous antebellum mansion before a few friends and family, Sunny McAdams-Rostam swallowed her pride and ate her words.

Fortunately, the kiss her new husband planted on her lips made the harried decision to jump headlong into wedded bliss seem completely worthwhile. So did the fact he looked incredible in a tuxedo. And he was rich as chocolate. So rich he'd bought her the house serving as the majestic background. Not that his money ever mattered, nor would it.

But that wealth did enable them to take an extended honeymoon in Milan following the ceremony, as suggested by Adan, who as Rayad's best man, now followed behind them as they walked back down the aisle, the matron of honor—her twin—on his arm.

When they passed the last row of chairs, Sunny leaned over to Rayad and whispered, "Do you think they have caves in Italy?"

"I am certain if they do, we will find them."

They shared a laugh as they strolled to the gazebo where the reception was being held. Once they arrived, they paused for a picture with the attendants, greeted a few guests then unfortunately parted ways when Adan took Rayad aside for an impromptu military conference.

Piper approached her then and gave her a hug. "You look fantastic in that wedding gown, Sunshine. Satin and strapless suit you well."

Sunny surveyed the bridesmaid gown from hem to neck. "You don't look so bad yourself, Pookie. And you said you couldn't wear red."

"I look like a large tomato," she said, her hand automatically going to her belly. "It's only going to get worse when I move into the second trimester."

She gave her sister a squeeze. "I can't wait to have another nephew or niece."

"I can't wait to stop throwing up morning, noon and night." Piper's features turned solemn. "Are you happy, Sunny?"

"I can't begin to tell you how happy I am. I never thought I would find anyone who is so much in sync with me, and in many ways, like me."

"So he's stubborn and bites everyone's head off in the morning?"

"Very funny, Pookie."

"Bite me, Sunshine."

"Honestly, I'd rather have something to eat. Lately I can't seem to get enough food."

Piper eyed her suspiciously. "Is there a reason for that?"

She should have known her twin would unearth her biggest secret. "Yes, there is, but I haven't told Rayad yet."

"You're going to have a baby, too?"

Sunny grabbed Piper's arm and pulled her away from the guests. "Please keep your voice down. I don't want to have to explain this to Nana and Poppa, and I sure don't want my husband to learn the news from a stranger before I have a chance to tell him."

"What news would that be?"

Sunny took her attention from her sister and gave it to said husband, who was standing to her left. "Just something I learned a couple of days ago."

Piper stepped back, a sheepish look on her face. "I believe that's my cue to give the bride and groom some alone time." She then had the nerve to give Rayad a hug and tell him, "Congratulations on the wedding, and what you're about to find out."

When Piper practically sprinted away, her low ponytail swinging in the March breeze, Rayad turned to Sunny, his face fraught with confusion. "Would you please tell me what she meant by that comment?"

She set her bouquet aside on a bench and hooked her arm through his. "Yes, I will gladly tell you, while we're taking a walk."

They took a stroll through the manicured gardens washed in gold due to the setting sun. "I still can't believe you gave me this place as a wedding gift," Sunny said after a time.

"Nothing is too good for my bride," he replied. "I personally cannot believe you continue to avoid telling me this news."

That would take a great deal of courage, and moving on to the topic slowly. "I've been thinking I'd like to put in a pool in the back of the house. It gets really hot in Atlanta during the summer, kind of like the desert."

"That is your news?"

She swallowed hard. "I'll get to that shortly. I've also been thinking the side yard would be a good place to put a play yard with swings and slides and maybe monkey bars. Of course, we'd wait until we get back from the honeymoon before we do that."

"Why would we need a play yard at this point in time?"

She lifted her bare shoulders in a shrug. "Well, Sam will be using it when Piper and Adan bring him for a visit. Zain and Madison would appreciate having a place for the twins to play when they come later this summer since they couldn't make the wedding. And of course, Rafiq and Maysa and their little boy will surely stop in at some point in time. Also, we'll need to add a baby swing for our son or daughter within the next year."

He stopped dead in his tracks and turned her toward him. "You would be willing to conceive a child within a year?"

The moment of truth had arrived. "We've already conceived a child, honey. That's my real news."

Myriad emotions passed over his face, beginning with puzzlement and ending with awareness. "You are pregnant."

"Yes, I am. About six weeks. And just so you're clear, I didn't plan this. I did forget to take my pills two days during all the wedding planning chaos." When he didn't offer a response, she grew worried. "How do you feel about this bombshell?"

"Concerned," he said. "Afraid."

Not at all what she'd wanted to hear. "What are you afraid of?"

"That I might not be able to keep you both safe at all times."

She formed her palm to his face. "Rayad, life doesn't come with guarantees, but mothers have babies every day without incident. Look at Maysa. She gave birth to a nine-pounder naturally. They're both doing fine."

"I understand that, yet I still cannot help but remember my failures."

She didn't have to ask about those presumed failures. "It's going to take time to work through this, honey, and I'll be there with you every step of the way. I only hope that when you hold our baby in your arms for the first time, you'll realize you've been given a second chance."

He clasped her hands and touched the band he had placed on her left finger less than an hour ago. "I promise you now I will not go back."

"To the military?"

"To that place where I became trapped in a hell of my own making. I will move forward with my life, as long as you are by my side. And I will endeavor to protect you to the best of my ability."

"No guns involved, I hope."

He finally smiled. "No more guns from this point forward."

"I love you, my sweet, strong husband. Always."

"As I love you, my beloved wife. For eternity."

After they sealed their commitment to each other with the second kiss of the evening, Sunny felt truly blessed to have found a really nice guy beneath that stoic exterior. Her remarkable lover. Her retired assassin. Her one true love, now and forevermore.

* * * * *

If you loved this novel, don't miss these other sexy sheikh stories from Kristi Gold:

ONE NIGHT WITH THE SHEIKH
THE SHEIKH'S SON
EXPECTING THE SHEIKH'S BABY
THE RETURN OF THE SHEIKH

Available now from Harlequin Desire!

COMING NEXT MONTH FROM

HARLEQUIN®

Desire

Available February 3, 2015

#2353 HER FORBIDDEN COWBOY
Moonlight Beach Bachelors • by Charlene Sands
When his late wife's younger sister needs a place to heal after being jilted at the altar, country-and-western star Zane Williams offers comfort at his beachfront mansion. But when he takes her in his arms, they enter forbidden territory...

#2354 HIS LOST AND FOUND FAMILY
Texas Cattleman's Club: After the Storm
by Sarah M. Anderson
Tracking down his estranged wife to their hometown hospital, entrepreneur Jake Holt discovers she's lost her memory—and had his baby. Will their renewed love stand the test when she remembers what drove them apart?

#2355 THE BLACKSTONE HEIR
Billionaires and Babies • by Dani Wade
Mill owner Jacob Blackstone is all business; bartender KC Gatlin goes with the flow. But her baby secret is about to shake things up as these two very different people come together for their child's future...and their own.

#2356 THIRTY DAYS TO WIN HIS WIFE
Brides and Belles • by Andrea Laurence
Thinking twice after a reckless Vegas elopement, two best friends find their divorce plans derailed by a surprise pregnancy. Will a relationship trial run prove they might be perfect partners, after all?

#2357 THE TEXAN'S ROYAL M.D.
Duchess Diaries • by Merline Lovelace
When a sexy doctor from a royal bloodline saves the nephew of a Texas billionaire, she loses her heart in the process. But secrets from her past may keep her from the man she loves...

#2358 TERMS OF A TEXAS MARRIAGE
by Lauren Canan
The fine print of a hundred-year-old land lease will dictate Shea Hardin's fate: she must marry a bully or lose it all. But what happens when she falls for her fake husband...hard?

YOU CAN FIND MORE INFORMATION ON UPCOMING HARLEQUIN® TITLES, FREE EXCERPTS AND MORE AT WWW.HARLEQUIN.COM.

HDCNM0115

REQUEST YOUR FREE BOOKS!
2 FREE NOVELS PLUS 2 FREE GIFTS!

HARLEQUIN®

Desire

ALWAYS POWERFUL, PASSIONATE AND PROVOCATIVE

YES! Please send me 2 FREE Harlequin Desire® novels and my 2 FREE gifts (gifts are worth about $10). After receiving them, if I don't wish to receive any more books, I can return the shipping statement marked "cancel." If I don't cancel, I will receive 6 brand-new novels every month and be billed just $4.55 per book in the U.S. or $4.99 per book in Canada. That's a savings of at least 13% off the cover price! It's quite a bargain! Shipping and handling is just 50¢ per book in the U.S. and 75¢ per book in Canada.* I understand that accepting the 2 free books and gifts places me under no obligation to buy anything. I can always return a shipment and cancel at any time. Even if I never buy another book, the two free books and gifts are mine to keep forever.

225/326 HDN F4ZC

Name _____ (PLEASE PRINT) _____

Address _____ Apt. #

City _____ State/Prov. _____ Zip/Postal Code

Signature (if under 18, a parent or guardian must sign)

Mail to the **Harlequin**® Reader Service:
IN U.S.A.: P.O. Box 1867, Buffalo, NY 14240-1867
IN CANADA: P.O. Box 609, Fort Erie, Ontario L2A 5X3

Want to try two free books from another line?
Call 1-800-873-8635 or visit www.ReaderService.com.

* Terms and prices subject to change without notice. Prices do not include applicable taxes. Sales tax applicable in N.Y. Canadian residents will be charged applicable taxes. Offer not valid in Quebec. This offer is limited to one order per household. Not valid for current subscribers to Harlequin Desire books. All orders subject to credit approval. Credit or debit balances in a customer's account(s) may be offset by any other outstanding balance owed by or to the customer. Please allow 4 to 6 weeks for delivery. Offer available while quantities last.

Your Privacy—The Harlequin® Reader Service is committed to protecting your privacy. Our Privacy Policy is available online at www.ReaderService.com or upon request from the Harlequin Reader Service.

We make a portion of our mailing list available to reputable third parties that offer products we believe may interest you. If you prefer that we not exchange your name with third parties, or if you wish to clarify or modify your communication preferences, please visit us at www.ReaderService.com/consumerschoice or write to us at Harlequin Reader Service Preference Service, P.O. Box 9062, Buffalo, NY 14269. Include your complete name and address.

HD13R

SPECIAL EXCERPT FROM

HARLEQUIN®

Desire

Here's a sneak peek at the next
**TEXAS CATTLEMAN'S CLUB:
AFTER THE STORM** installment,
HIS LOST AND FOUND FAMILY
by *Sarah M. Anderson*

*Separated and on the verge of divorce, Jake Holt is
determined to confront his wife. But when he arrives
in Royal, Texas, he finds that Skye has been keeping
secrets...*

Jake had spent the past four years pointedly not caring
about what his family was doing. They'd wanted him to
put the family above his wife. Nothing had been more
important to him than Skye.

He was not staying in Royal long. Just enough to get
Skye back on her feet and figure out where they stood.

Just then, the baby made a little hiccup-sigh noise that
pulled at his heartstrings.

Jake's brother picked the baby up so smoothly that
Jake was jealous.

"Grace, honey—this is your daddy," Keaton said as he
rubbed her back. Then, to Jake, he added, "You ready?"

Not really—but Jake wasn't going to admit that to
Keaton. He tried to cradle his arms in the right way. Then
Keaton laid the baby in them.

The world seemed to tilt off its axis as Jake looked
down into his daughter's eyes. They were a pale blue—